## "I LIKE A GOOD DETECTIVE STORY,"

said the venerable Mr. Treves.

"But, you know, they begin in the wrong place! They begin with the murder. But the murder is the *end*. The story begins long before that—years before, sometimes—with all the causes and events that bring certain people to a certain place at a certain time on a certain day. All converging towards a given spot. . . . And then, when the time comes—over the top! *Zero hour*."

He sat down in front of the fire and reflected on the events of the day.

"Even now," he thought, "some drama is in the course of preparation. If I were writing one of these amusing stories of blood and crime, I should begin now with an elderly gentleman sitting in front of the fire opening his letters—going, unbeknownst to himself, towards zero. . . ."

## Books by Agatha Christie

The A.B.C. Murders
At Bertram's Hotel
The Body in the Library
By the Pricking of My Thumbs
A Caribbean Mystery
Cat Among the Pigeons
The Clocks
Come, Tell Me How You Live
Crooked House
Curtain
Dead Man's Folly
Death Comes as the End
Easy to Kill (Original British title: Murder Is Easy)
Endless Night
Evil Under the Sun
Funerals Are Fatal
Hallowe'en Party
Hickory Dickory Death (Original British title: Hickory, Dickory, Dock)
The Mirror Crack'd (Original British title: The Mirror Crack'd from Side to Side)
Mrs. McGinty's Dead
A Murder Is Announced
The Murder of Roger Ackroyd

Murder on the Orient Express (Also published as Murder in The Calais Coach)
Murder with Mirrors (Original British title: They Do It with Mirrors)
The Mystery of the Blue Train
Nemesis
Ordeal by Innocence
The Pale Horse
Passenger to Frankfurt
Peril at End House
A Pocket Full of Rye
Remembered Death (Original British title: Sparkling Cyanide)
So Many Steps to Death (Original British title: Destination Unknown)
Ten Little Indians (Also published as And Then There Were None)
Third Girl
Towards Zero
What Mrs. McGillicuddy Saw (Original British title: 4:50 from Paddington)

Published by POCKET BOOKS

# Agatha Christie
# Towards Zero

PUBLISHED BY POCKET BOOKS NEW YORK

Distributed in Canada by PaperJacks Ltd., a Licensee
of the trademarks of Simon & Schuster, a division of
Gulf+Western Corporation.

POCKET BOOKS, a Simon & Schuster division of
GULF & WESTERN CORPORATION
1230 Avenue of the Americas, New York, N.Y. 10020
In Canada distributed by PaperJacks Ltd.,
330 Steelcase Road, Markham, Ontario.

Published by arrangement with Dodd, Mead & Company

ISBN: 0-671-43464-0

First Pocket Books printing January, 1947

35   34   33   32   31   30

POCKET and colophon are trademarks of Simon & Schuster.

Printed in Canada

# CONTENTS

# CAST OF CHARACTERS

MR. TREVES—A ripe and experienced solicitor of eighty whose excellent memory for past murders proved to be the death of him

ANDREW MACWHIRTER—A complete down-and-outer rescued unwillingly from an attempted suicide, he happened to be on the spot some months later to perform the same service for a damsel in distress

SUPERINTENDENT BATTLE—Scotland Yard's poker-faced detective discovered that his methodical sleuthing stood him in good stead, even on his vacation

MISS AMPHREY—Successful headmistress of a girls' school, she was an excellent example of the danger of half-baked psychological theories in the head of an amateur

SYLVIA BATTLE—The Superintendent's young daughter, her painful boarding-school experience helped him clear an innocent victim

NEVILE STRANGE—A veritable Apollo, he had everything a man could ask for, including a wide reputation as an excellent athlete, a large bank account and two beautiful wives—yet he wasn't happy

KAY STRANGE—Young and vibrantly alive, with a temper that nearly matched her matchless red hair—definitely not the sort to play second fiddle to Nevile's first wife

LADY CAMILLA TRESSILIAN—The autocratic invalid enjoyed entertaining immensely, but she drew the line when Gull's Point suddenly became converted to a *ménage à trois*

MARY ALDIN—Self-sacrificing, devoted companion to the aging Lady Camilla, she enjoyed her position as arbitrator for a houseful of edgy guests—until it became too much for even *her* gentle patience

AUDREY STRANGE—Her shimmering, mothlike beauty pervaded Gull's Point, distracting Nevile Strange and infuriating his latest spouse

THOMAS ROYDE—Known as "True Thomas" to his adopted sister Audrey, he harbored a passionate heart beneath his seemingly phlegmatic indifference

TED LATIMER—The handsome young "boyhood chum" of Kay Strange's was forever popping up in her immediate vicinity

INSPECTOR JAMES LEACH—Battle's nephew, assigned to the case of murder at Gull's Point and new at his post, he enlisted his uncle's aid and thereby learned a number of useful lessons

# PROLOGUE

*November 19th*

THE GROUP round the fireplace was nearly all composed of lawyers or those who had an interest in the law. There was Martindale, the solicitor; Rufus Lord, K.C.; young Daniels, who had made a name for himself in the Carstairs case; a sprinkling of other barristers —Mr. Justice Cleaver, Lewis of Lewis and Trench and old Mr. Treves. Mr. Treves was close on eighty, a very ripe and experienced eighty. He was a member of a famous firm of solicitors, and the most famous member of that firm. He had settled innumerable delicate cases out of court, he was said to know more of backstairs history than any man in England and he was a specialist on criminology.

Unthinking people said Mr. Treves ought to write his memoirs. Mr. Treves knew better. He knew that he knew too much.

Though he had long retired from active practice, there was no man in England whose opinion was so respected by the members of his own fraternity. Whenever his thin, precise, little voice was raised there was always a respectful silence.

The conversation now was on the subject of a much talked of case which had finished that day at the Old Bailey. It was a murder case and the prisoner had been acquitted. The present company was busy trying the case over again and making technical criticisms.

The prosecution had made a mistake in relying on one of its witnesses—old Depleach ought to have realized what an opening he was giving to the defense. Young Arthur had made the most of that servant girl's evidence. Bentmore, in his summing up, had very rightly put the matter in its correct perspective, but the mischief was done by then—the jury had believed the girl. Juries were funny—you never knew what they'd swallow and what they wouldn't—but let them once get a thing into their heads and no one was ever going to get it out again. They believed that the girl was speaking the truth about the crowbar and that was that. The medical evidence had been a bit above their heads. All those long terms and scientific jargon—damned bad witnesses, these scientific johnnies—always hemmed and hawed and couldn't say yes or no to a plain question—always "under certain circumstances that might take place"—and so on!

They talked themselves out, little by little, and as the remarks became more spasmodic and disjointed, a general feeling grew of something lacking. One head after another turned in the direction of Mr. Treves. For Mr. Treves had as yet contributed nothing to the discussion. Gradually it became apparent that the company were waiting for a final word from their most respected colleague.

Mr. Treves, leaning back in his chair, was absent-mindedly polishing his glasses. Something in the silence made him look up sharply.

"Eh?" he said. "What was that? You asked me something?"

Young Lewis spoke:

"We were talking, sir, about the Lamorne case."

He paused expectantly.

"Yes, yes," said Mr. Treves. "I was thinking of that."

There was a respectful hush.

"But I'm afraid," said Mr. Treves, still polishing, "that I was being fanciful. Yes, fanciful. Result of getting on in years, I suppose. At my age one can claim the privilege of being fanciful, if one likes."

"Yes, indeed, sir," said young Lewis, but he looked puzzled.

"I was thinking," said Mr. Treves, "not so much of the various points of law raised—though they were interesting—very interesting—if the verdict had gone the other way there would have been good grounds for appeal, I rather think—but I won't go into that now. I was thinking, as I say, not of the points of law but of the—well, of the *people* in the case."

Everybody looked rather astonished. They had considered the people in the case only as regarded their credibility or otherwise as witnesses. None of them had even hazarded a speculation as to whether the prisoner had been guilty or as innocent as the court had pronounced him to be.

"Human beings, you know," said Mr. Treves thoughtfully. "Human beings. All kinds and sorts and sizes and shapes of 'em. Some with brains and a good many more without. They'd come from all over the place, Lancashire, Scotland—that restaurant proprietor from Italy, and that schoolteacher woman from somewhere out Middle West. All caught up and enmeshed in the thing

and finally all brought together in a court of law in
London on a grey November day. Each one contribut-
ing his little part. The whole thing culminating in a
trial for murder."

He paused and gently beat a delicate tattoo on his
knee.

"I like a good detective story," he said. "But, you
know, they begin in the wrong place! They begin with
the murder. But the murder is the *end*. The story begins long before that—years before sometimes—with all
the causes and events that bring certain people to a
certain place at a certain time on a certain day. Take
that little maid servant's evidence—if the kitchenmaid
hadn't pinched her young man she wouldn't have thrown
up her situation in a huff and gone to the Lamornes
and been the principal witness for the defense. That
Giuseppe Antonelli—coming over to exchange with his
brother for a month. The brother is as blind as a bat.
He wouldn't have seen what Giuseppe's sharp eyes saw.
If the constable hadn't been sweet on the cook at No.
48, *he* wouldn't have been late on his beat. . . ."

He nodded his head gently.

"All converging towards a given spot. . . . And then,
when the time comes—over the top! *Zero hour*. Yes,
all of them converging towards zero. . . ."

He repeated, "Towards zero. . . ."

Then he gave a quick little shudder.

"You're cold, sir, come nearer the fire."

"No, no," said Mr. Treves. "Just someone walking
over my grave as they say. Well, well, I must be making
my way homewards."

He gave an affable little nod and went slowly and
precisely out of the room.

There was a moment's dubious silence and then Rufus
Lord, K.C., remarked that poor old Treves was getting
on.

Sir William Cleaver said:

"An acute brain—a very acute brain—but anno domini tells in the end."

"Got a groggy heart, too," said Lord. "May drop down any minute I believe."

"He takes pretty good care of himself," said young Lewis.

At that moment Mr. Treves was carefully stepping into his smooth-running Daimler. It deposited him at a house in a quiet square. A solicitous butler valet helped him off with his coat. Mr. Treves walked into his library where a coal fire was burning. His bedroom lay beyond, for out of consideration for his heart he never went upstairs.

He sat down in front of the fire and drew his letters towards him.

His mind was still dwelling on the fancy he had outlined at the Club.

"Even now," thought Mr. Treves to himself, "some drama—some murder to be—is in course of preparation. If I were writing one of these amusing stories of blood and crime, I should begin now with an elderly gentleman sitting in front of the fire opening his letters—going, unbeknownst to himself—towards zero. . . ."

He slit open an envelope and gazed down absently at the sheet he extracted from it.

Suddenly his expression changed. He came back from romance to reality.

"Dear me," said Mr. Treves. "How extremely annoying! Really, how very vexing. After all these years! This will alter all my plans."

# "OPEN THE DOOR AND HERE ARE THE PEOPLE"

*January 11th*

THE MAN in the hospital bed shifted his body slightly and stifled a groan.

The nurse in charge of the ward got up from her table and came down to him. She shifted his pillows and moved him into a more comfortable position.

Andrew MacWhirter only gave a grunt by way of thanks.

He was in a state of seething rebellion and bitterness.

By this time it ought all to have been over. He ought to have been out of it all! Curse that damned ridiculous tree growing out of the cliff! Curse those officious sweethearts who braved the cold of a winter's night to keep a tryst on the cliff edge.

But for them (and the tree!) it *would* have been over —a plunge into the deep icy water, a brief struggle perhaps, and then oblivion—the end of a misused, useless, unprofitable life.

And now where was he? Lying ridiculously in a hospital bed with a broken shoulder and with the prospect of being hauled up in a police court for the crime of trying to take his own life.

Curse it, it was his *own* life, wasn't it?

And if he had succeeded in the job, they would have buried him piously as of unsound mind!

Unsound mind, indeed! He'd never been saner! And to commit suicide was the most logical and sensible thing that could be done by a man in his position.

Completely down and out, with his health permanently affected, with a wife who had left him for another man. Without a job, without affection, without money, health or hope, surely to end it all was the only possible solution?

And now here he was in this ridiculous plight. He would shortly be admonished by a sanctimonious magistrate for doing the common sense thing with a commodity which belonged to him and to him only—his life.

He snorted with anger. A wave of fever passed over him.

The nurse was beside him again.

She was young, red-haired, with a kindly, rather vacant face.

"Are you in much pain?"

"No, I'm not."

"I'll give you something to make you sleep."

"You'll do nothing of the sort."

"But—"

"Do you think I can't bear a bit of pain and sleeplessness?"

She smiled in a gentle, slightly superior way.

"Doctor said you could have something."

"I don't care what doctor said."

She straightened the covers and set a glass of lemonade a little nearer to him. He said, slightly ashamed of himself, "Sorry if I was rude."

"Oh, that's all right."

It annoyed him that she was so completely undisturbed by his bad temper. Nothing like that could penetrate her nurse's armor of indulgent indifference. He was a patient—not a man.

He said:

"Damned interference—all this damned interference . . ."

She said reprovingly, "Now, now, that isn't very nice."

"Nice?" he demanded. *"Nice?* My God."

She said calmly, "You'll feel better in the morning."

He swallowed.

"You nurses. You *nurses!* You're inhuman, that's what you are!"

"We know what's best for you, you see."

"That's what's so infuriating! About you. About a hospital. About the world. Continual interference! Knowing what's best for other people. I tried to kill myself. You know that, don't you?"

She nodded.

"Nobody's business but mine whether I threw myself off a bloody cliff or not. I'd finished with life. I was down and out!"

She made a little clicking noise with her tongue. It indicated abstract sympathy. He was a patient. She was soothing him by letting him blow off steam.

"Why shouldn't I kill myself if I want to?" he demanded.

She replied to that quite seriously.

"Because it's wrong."

"Why is it wrong?"

She looked at him doubtfully. She was not disturbed

in her own belief, but she was much too inarticulate to explain her reaction.

"Well—I mean—it's wicked to kill yourself. You've got to go on living whether you like it or not."

"Why have you?"

"Well, there are other people to consider, aren't there?"

"Not in my case. There's not a soul in the world who'd be the worse for my passing on."

"Haven't you got any relations? No mother or sister or anything?"

"No. I had a wife once but she left me—quite right too! She saw I was no good."

"But you've got friends, surely?"

"No, I haven't. I'm not a friendly sort of man. Look here, nurse, I'll tell you something. I was a happy sort of chap once. Had a good job and a good-looking wife. There was a car accident. My boss was driving the car and I was in it. He wanted me to say he was driving under thirty at the time of the accident. He wasn't. He was driving nearer fifty. Nobody was killed, nothing like that, he just wanted to be in the right for the insurance people. Well, I wouldn't say what he wanted. It was a lie. I don't tell lies."

The nurse said, "Well, I think you were quite right. Quite right."

"You do, do you? That pigheadedness of mine cost me my job. My boss was sore. He saw to it that I didn't get another. My wife got fed up seeing me mooch about unable to get anything to do. She went off with a man who had been my friend. He was doing well and going up in the world. I drifted along going steadily down. I took to drinking a bit. That didn't help me to hold down jobs. Finally I came down to hauling—strained my inside—the doctor told me I'd never be strong again. Well, there wasn't much to live for then. Easiest way, and the cleanest way, was to go right out. My life was no good to myself or anyone else."

The little nurse murmured, "You don't know that."

He laughed. He was better tempered already. Her naïve obstinacy amused him.

"My dear girl, what use am I to anybody?"

She said confusedly, "You don't know. You may be—someday—"

"Someday? There won't be any someday. Next time I shall make sure."

She shook her head decidedly.

"Oh, no," she said. "You won't kill yourself now."

"Why not?"

"They never do."

He stared at her: *"They never do."* He was one of a class of would-be suicides. Opening his mouth to protest energetically, his innate honesty suddenly stopped him.

*Would* he do it again? Did he really mean to do it?

He knew suddenly that he didn't. For no reason. Perhaps the right reason was the one she had given out of her specialized knowledge. Suicides didn't do it again.

All the more he felt determined to force an admission from her on the ethical side.

"At any rate I've got a right to do what I like with my own life."

"No—no, you haven't."

"But why not, my dear girl, why?"

She flushed. She said, her fingers playing with the little gold cross that hung round her neck:

"You don't understand. God may need you."

He stared—taken aback. He did not want to upset her childlike faith. He said mockingly:

"I suppose that one day I may stop a runaway horse and save a golden-haired child from death—eh? Is that it?"

She shook her head. She said with vehemence and trying to express what was so vivid in her mind and so halting on her tongue:

"It may be just by *being* somewhere—not doing anything—just by being at a certain place at a certain time —oh, I can't say what I mean, but you might just— just walk along a street someday and just by doing that accomplish something terribly important—perhaps without even knowing what it was."

The red-haired little nurse came from the west coast of Scotland and some of her family had "the sight."

Perhaps, dimly, she saw a picture of a man walking up a road on a night in September and thereby saving a human being from a terrible death. . . .


*February 14th*


THERE WAS only one person in the room and the only sound to be heard was the scratching of that person's pen as it traced line after line across the paper.

There was no one to read the words that were being traced. If there had been, they would hardly have believed their eyes. For what was being written was a clear, carefully detailed project for murder.

There are times when a body is conscious of a mind controlling it—when it bows obedient to that alien something that controls its actions. There are other times when a mind is conscious of owning and controlling a body and accomplishing its purpose by using that body.

The figure sitting writing was in the last named state. It was a mind, a cool controlled intelligence. This mind had only one thought and one purpose—the destruction of another human being. To the end that his purpose might be accomplished, the scheme was being worked out meticulously on paper. Every eventuality, every possibility was being taken into account. The thing had got to be absolutely foolproof. The scheme, like all good schemes, was not absolutely cut and dried. There were certain alternative actions at certain points. Moreover, since the mind was intelligent, it realized that there must be intelligent provision left for the unforeseen. But the main lines were clear and had been closely tested. The time, the place, the method, the victim! . . .

The figure raised its head. With its hand, it picked up the sheets of paper and read them carefully through. Yes, the thing was crystal clear.

Across the serious face a smile came. It was a smile that was not quite sane. The figure drew a deep breath.

As man was made in the image of his maker, so there was now a terrible travesty of a creator's joy.

Yes, everything planned—everyone's reaction foretold and allowed for, the good and evil in everybody played upon and brought into harmony with one evil design.

There was one thing lacking still. . . .

With a smile the writer traced a date—a date in September.

Then, with a laugh, the paper was torn in pieces and the pieces carried across the room and put into the heart of the glowing fire. There was no carelessness. Every single piece was consumed and destroyed. The plan was now only existent in the brain of its creator.

*March 8th*

SUPERINTENDENT BATTLE was sitting at the breakfast table. His jaw was set in a truculent fashion and he was reading slowly and carefully a letter that his wife had just tearfully handed to him. There was no expres-

sion visible on his face, for his face never did register
any expression. It had the aspect of a face carved out
of wood. It was solid and durable and, in some way,
impressive. Superintendent Battle had never suggested
brilliance; he was, definitely, not a brilliant man, but
he had some other quality, difficult to define, that was
nevertheless forceful.

"I can't believe it," said Mrs. Battle, sobbing. "Sylvia!"

Sylvia was the youngest of Superintendent and Mrs.
Battle's five children. She was sixteen and at school near
Maidstone.

The letter was from Miss Amphrey, headmistress of
the school in question. It was a clear, kindly and extremely tactful letter. It set out, in black and white, that
various small thefts had been puzzling the school au-
thorities for some time, that the matter had been at last
cleared up, that Sylvia Battle had confessed and that
Miss Amphrey would like to see Mr. and Mrs. Battle at
the earliest possible opportunity "to discuss the position."

Superintendent Battle folded up the letter, put it in
his pocket, and said, "You leave this to me, Mary."

He got up, walked round the table, patted her on the
cheek and said, "Don't worry, dear, it will be all right."

He went from the room leaving comfort and re-
assurance behind him.

That afternoon, in Miss Amphrey's modern and indi-
vidualistic drawing room, Superintendent Battle sat very
squarely on his chair, his large wooden hands on his
knees, confronting Miss Amphrey and managing to
look, far more than usual, every inch a policeman.

Miss Amphrey was a very successful headmistress.
She had personality—a great deal of personality, she
was enlightened and up to date, and she combined dis-
cipline with modern ideas of self-determination.

Her room was representative of the spirit of Mead-
way. Everything was of a cool oatmeal color—there were
big jars of daffodils and bowls of tulips and hyacinths.
One or two good copies of the antique Greek, two pieces
of advanced modern sculpture, two Italian primitives
on the walls. In the midst of all this, Miss Amphrey
herself, dressed in a deep shade of blue, with an eager
face suggestive of a conscientious greyhound, and clear
blue eyes looking serious through thick lenses.

"The important thing," she was saying in her clear,
well-modulated voice, "is that this should be taken the
right way. It is the girl herself we have to think of, Mr.
Battle. Sylvia herself! It is more important—*most* important—that her life should not be crippled in any
way. She must not be made to assume a burden of *guilt*
—blame must be very very sparingly meted out, if at
all. We must arrive at the reason *behind* these quite
trivial pilferings. A sense of inferiority, perhaps? She
is not good at games, you know—an obscure wish to
shine in a different sphere—the desire to assert her ego?
We must be very very careful. That is why I wanted
to see you alone first—to impress upon you to be very,
very careful with Sylvia. I repeat again, it's very important to get at what is *behind* this."

"That, Miss Amphrey," said Superintendent Battle,
"is why I have come down."

His voice was quiet, his face unemotional, his eyes
surveyed the schoolmistress appraisingly.

"I have been very gentle with her," said Miss Amphrey.

Battle said laconically, "Good of you, m'am."

"You see, I really love and understand these young
things."

Battle did not reply directly. He said, "I'd like to
see my girl now, if you don't mind, Miss Amphrey."

With renewed emphasis Miss Amphrey admonished

him to be careful—to go slow—not to antagonize a child just budding into womanhood.

Superintendent Battle showed no signs of impatience. He just looked blank.

She took him at last to her study. They passed one or two girls in the passages. They stood politely to attention but their eyes were full of curiosity. Having ushered Battle into a small room not quite so redolent of personality as the one downstairs, Miss Amphrey withdrew and said she would send Sylvia to him.

Just as she was leaving the room, Battle stopped her.

"One minute, m'am, how did you come to pitch upon Sylvia as the one responsible for these—er—leakages?"

"My methods, Mr. Battle, were psychological."

Miss Amphrey spoke with dignity.

"Psychological? H'm. What about the evidence, Miss Amphrey?"

"Yes, yes, I quite understand, Mr. Battle—you would feel that way. Your—er—profession steps in. But psychology is beginning to be recognized in criminology. I can assure you that there is no mistake—Sylvia freely admits the whole thing."

Battle nodded.

"Yes, yes—I know that. I was just asking how you came to pitch upon her to begin with."

"Well, Mr. Battle, this business of things being taken out of the girls' lockers was on the increase. I called the school together and told them the facts. At the same time, I studied their faces unobtrusively. Slyvia's expression struck me at once. It was guilty—confused. I knew at that moment who was responsible. I wanted, not to *confront* her with her guilt, but to get her to admit it *herself*. I set a little test for her—a word association test."

Battle nodded to show he understood.

"And finally the child admitted it all!"

Her father said, "I see."

Miss Amphrey hesitated a minute, then went out.

Battle was standing looking out of the window when the door opened again.

He turned round slowly and looked at his daughter.

Sylvia stood just inside the door which she had closed behind her. She was tall, dark, angular. Her face was sullen and bore marks of tears. She said timidly rather than defiantly:

"Well, here I am."

Battle looked at her thoughtfully for a minute or two. He sighed.

"I should never have sent you to this place," he said. "That woman's a fool."

Sylvia lost sight of her own problem in sheer amazement.

"Miss Amphrey? Oh, but she's *wonderful!* We all think so."

"H'm," said Battle. "Can't be quite a fool, then, if she sells the idea of herself as well as that. All the same, this wasn't the place for you—although I don't know —this might have happened anywhere."

Sylvia twisted her hands together. She looked down. She said,

"I'm—I'm sorry, Father. I really am."

"So you should be," said Battle shortly. "Come here."

She came slowly and unwillingly across the room to him. He took her chin in his great square hand and looked closely into her face.

"Been through a great deal, haven't you?" he said gently.

Tears started into her eyes.

Battle said slowly:

"You see, Sylvia, I've known all along with you, that there was *something*. Most people have got a weakness of some kind or another. Usually it's plain enough. You can see when a child's greedy, or bad tempered, or got a streak of the bully in him. You were a good child, very quiet—very sweet tempered—no trouble in any way—and sometimes I've worried. Because if there's a flaw you don't see, sometimes it wrecks the whole show when the article is tried out."

"Like me!" said Sylvia.

"Yes, like you. You've cracked under strain—and in a damned queer way too. It's a way, oddly enough, I've never come across before."

The girl said suddenly and scornfully:

"I should think you'd come across thieves often enough!"

"Oh, yes—I know all about them. And that's why, my dear—not because I'm your father (fathers don't know much about their children) but because I'm a *policeman* that I know well enough you're not a thief! *You* never took a thing in this place. Thieves are of two kinds, the kind that yields to sudden and overwhelming temptation (and that happens damned seldom—it's amazing what temptation the ordinary normal honest human being can withstand), and there's the kind that just takes what doesn't belong to them almost as a matter of course. You don't belong to either type. You're not a thief. You're a very unusual type of liar."

Sylvia began: "But—"

He swept on.

"You've admitted it all? Oh, yes, I know *that*. There was a saint once—went out with bread for the poor. Husband didn't like it. Met her and asked what there was in her basket. She lost her nerve and said it was roses—He tore open her basket and roses it was—a miracle! Now if you'd been Saint Elizabeth and were out with a basket of roses, and your husband had come along and asked you what you'd got, you'd have lost your nerve and said 'Bread.' "

He paused and then said gently, "That's how it happened, isn't it?"

There was a longer pause and then the girl suddenly bent her head.

Battle said:

"Tell me, child. What happened exactly?"

"She had us all up. Made a speech. And I saw her eyes on me and I knew she thought it was me! I felt myself getting red—and I saw some of the girls looking at me. It was awful. And then the others began looking at me and whispering in corners. I could see they all thought so. And then the Amp had me up here with some of the others one evening and we played a sort of word game—she said words and we gave answers—"

Battle gave a disgusted grunt.

"And I could see what it meant—and—and I sort of got paralyzed. I tried not to give the wrong word—I tried to think of things quite outside—like squirrels or flowers—and the Amp was there watching me with eyes like gimlets—you know, sort of boring inside one. And after that—oh, it got worse and worse and one day the Amp talked to me quite kindly and so—so *understandingly*—and—and I broke down and said I *had* done it—and oh! Daddy, the relief!"

Battle was stroking his chin.

"I see."

"You do understand?"

"No, Sylvia, I don't understand, because I'm not made that way. If anyone tried to make me say I'd done something I hadn't I'd feel more like giving them a sock on the jaw. But I see how it came about in your case—and that gimlet-eyed Amp of yours has had as pretty an example of unusual psychology shoved under her nose as any half baked exponent of misunderstood theories could ask for. The thing to do now is to clear up this mess. Where's Miss Amphrey?"

Miss Amphrey was hovering tactfully near at hand. Her sympathetic smile froze on her face as Superintendent Battle said bluntly:

"In justice to my daughter, I must ask that you call in your local police over this."

"But, Mr. Battle, Sylvia herself—"

"Sylvia has never touched a thing that didn't belong to her in this place."

"I quite understand that, as a father—"

"I'm not talking as a father, but as a policeman. Get the police to give you a hand over this. They'll be discreet. You'll find the things hidden away somewhere and the right set of fingerprints on them, I expect. Petty pilferers don't think of wearing gloves. I'm taking my daughter away with me now. If the police find evidence —*real* evidence—to connect her with the thefts, I'm prepared for her to appear in court and take what's coming to her, but I'm not afraid."

As he drove out of the gate with Sylvia beside him some five minutes later, he asked, "Who's the girl with fair hair, rather fuzzy, very pink cheeks and a spot on her chin, blue eyes far apart? I passed her in the passage."

"That sounds like Olive Parsons."

"Ah, well, I shouldn't be surprised if she were the one."

"Did she look frightened?"

"No, looked smug! Calm smug look I've seen in the police court hundreds of times! I'd bet good money she's the thief—but you won't find *her* confessing—not much!"

Sylvia said with a sigh, "It's like coming out of a bad dream. Oh, Daddy, I am sorry! Oh, I *am* sorry! How could I be such a fool, such an utter fool? I do feel awful about it."

"Ah, well," said Superintendent Battle, patting her

on the arm with a hand he disengaged from the wheel, and uttering one of his pet forms of trite consolation, "don't you worry. These things are sent to try us. Yes, these things are sent to try us. At least, I suppose so. I don't see what else they can be sent for. . . ."


## April 19th

THE SUN was pouring down on Nevile Strange's house at Hindhead.

It was an April day such as usually occurs at least once in the month, hotter than most of the June days to follow.

Nevile Strange was coming down the stairs. He was dressed in white flannels and held four tennis rackets under his arm.

If a man could have been selected from amongst other Englishmen as an example of a lucky man with nothing to wish for, a Selection Committee might have chosen Nevile Strange. He was a man well known to the British public, a first-class tennis player and all-round sportsman. Though he had never reached the finals at Wimbledon, he had lasted several of the opening rounds and in the mixed doubles had twice reached the semifinals. He was, perhaps, too much of an all-round athlete to be a champion tennis player. He was scratch at golf, a fine swimmer and had done some good climbs in the Alps. He was thirty-three, had magnificent health, good looks, plenty of money, an extremely beautiful wife whom he had recently married and, to all appearances, no cares or worries.

Nevertheless as Nevile Strange went downstairs this fine morning a shadow went with him. A shadow perceptible, perhaps, to no eyes but his. But he was aware of it, the thought of it furrowed his brow and made his expression troubled and indecisive.

He crossed the hall, squared his shoulders as though definitely throwing off some burden, passed through the living room and out onto a glass verandah where his wife, Kay, was curled up amongst cushions drinking orange juice.

Kay Strange was twenty-three and unusually beautiful. She had a slender but subtly voluptuous figure, dark red hair, such a perfect skin that she used only the slightest of make-up to enhance it, and those dark eyes and brows which so seldom go with red hair and which are so devastating when they do.

Her husband said lightly:

"Hullo, gorgeous, what's for breakfast?"

Kay replied:

"Horribly bloody-looking kidneys for you—and mushrooms—and rolls of bacon."

"Sounds all right," said Nevile.

He helped himself to the aforementioned viands and poured out a cup of coffee. There was a companionable silence for some minutes.

"Oo," said Kay, voluptuously wriggling bare toes with scarlet manicured nails. "Isn't the sun lovely? England's not so bad after all."

They had just come back from the south of France.

Nevile, after a bare glance at the newspaper headlines, had turned to the sports page and merely said "Um . . ."

Then, proceeding to toast and marmalade, he put the paper aside and opened his letters.

There were a good many of these but most of them he tore across and chucked away. Circulars, advertisements, printed matter.

Kay said:

"I don't like my color scheme in the living room. Can I have it done over, Nevile?"

"Anything you like, beautiful."

"Peacock blue," said Kay dreamily. "And ivory satin cushions."

"You'll have to throw in an ape," said Nevile.

"You can be the ape," said Kay.

Nevile opened another letter.

"Oh, by the way," said Kay. "Shirty has asked us to go to Norway on the yacht at the end of June. Rather sickening we can't."

She looked cautiously sideways at Nevile and added wistfully: "I would love it so."

Something, some cloud, some uncertainty, seemed hovering on Nevile's face.

Kay said rebelliously:

"Have we *got* to go to dreary old Camilla's?"

Nevile frowned.

"Of course we have. Look here, Kay, we've had this out before. Sir Matthew was my guardian. He and Camilla looked after me. Gull's Point is my home, as far as any place is home to me."

"Oh, all right, all right," said Kay. "If we must, we must. After all we get all that money when she dies, so I suppose we have to suck up a bit."

Nevile said angrily:

"It's not a question of sucking up! She's no control over the money. Sir Matthew left it in trust for her during her lifetime and to come to me and my wife afterwards. It's a question of *affection*. Why can't you understand that?"

Kay said, after a moment's pause:

"I do understand really. I'm just putting on an act because—well, because I know I'm only allowed there on sufferance as it were. They hate me! Yes, they do! Lady Tressilian looks down that long nose of hers at me and Mary Aldin looks over my shoulder when she talks to me. It's all very well for *you*. You don't see what goes on."

"They always seem to me very polite to you. You know quite well I wouldn't stand for it if they weren't."

Kay gave him a curious look from under her dark lashes.

"They're polite enough. But they know how to get under my skin all right. I'm the interloper, that's what they feel."

"Well," said Nevile, "after all, I suppose—that's natural enough, isn't it?"

His voice had changed slightly. He got up and stood looking out at the view with his back to Kay.

"Oh, yes, I daresay it's natural. They were devoted to Audrey, weren't they?" Her voice shook a little. "Dear, well-bred, cool, colorless Audrey! Camilla's not forgiven me for taking her place."

Nevile did not turn. His voice was lifeless, dull. He said: "After all, Camilla's old—past seventy. Her generation doesn't really like divorce, you know. On the whole I think she's accepted the position very well considering how fond she was of—of Audrey."

His voice changed just a little as he spoke the name.

"They think you treated her badly."

"So I did," said Nevile under his breath, but his wife heard.

"Oh, Nevile—don't be so stupid. Just because she chose to make such a frightful fuss."

"She didn't make a fuss. Audrey never made fusses."

"Well, you know what I mean. Because she went away and was ill, and went about everywhere looking broken-hearted. That's what I call a fuss! Audrey's not what I call a good loser. From my point of view if a wife can't hold her husband she ought to give him up gracefully! You two had nothing in common. She never played a

game and was as anemic and washed up as—as a dish
rag. No life or go in her! If she really cared about you,
she ought to have thought about your happiness first
and been glad you were going to be happy with someone more suited to you."

Nevile turned. A faintly sardonic smile played round
his lips.

"What a little sportsman! How to play the game in
love and matrimony!"

Kay laughed and reddened.

"Well, perhaps I was going a bit far. But at any rate
once the thing had happened, there it was. You've got
to accept these things!"

Nevile said quietly, "Audrey accepted it. She divorced
me so that you and I could marry."

"Yes, I know—" Kay hesitated.

Nevile said:

"You've never understood Audrey."

"No, I haven't. In a way, Audrey gives me the creeps.
I don't know what it is about her. You never know what
she's thinking. . . . She's—she's a little frightening."

"Oh! nonsense, Kay."

"Well, she frightens *me*. Perhaps it's because she's
got brains."

"My lovely nitwit!"

Kay laughed.

"You always call me that!"

"Because it's what you are!"

They smiled at each other. Nevile came over to her
and, bending down, kissed the back of her neck.

"Lovely, lovely Kay," he murmured.

"Very good Kay," said Kay. "Giving up a lovely
yachting trip to go and be snubbed by her husband's
prim Victorian relations."

Nevile went back and sat down by the table.

"You know," he said, "I don't see why we shouldn't

go on that trip with Shirty if you really want to so much."

Kay sat up in astonishment.

"And what about Saltcreek and Gull's Point?"

Nevile said in a rather unnatural voice:

"I don't see why we shouldn't go there early in September."

"Oh, but, Nevile, surely——" She stopped.

"We can't go in July and August because of the Tournaments," said Nevile. "But we finish up at St. Loo the last week in August and it would fit in very well if we went on to Saltcreek from there."

"Oh, it would fit in all right—beautifully. But I thought—well, *she* always goes there for September, doesn't she?"

"Audrey, you mean?"

"Yes, I suppose they could put her off, but——"

"Why should they put her off?"

Kay stared at him dubiously.

"You mean, we'd be there at the same time? What an extraordinary idea."

Nevile said irritably:

"I don't think it's at all an extraordinary idea. Lots of people do it nowadays. Why shouldn't we all be friends together? It makes things so much *simpler*. Why, you said so yourself only the other day."

"*I* did?"

"Yes, don't you remember? We were talking about the Howes, and you said it was the sensible civilized way to look at things, and that Leonard's new wife and his Ex were the best of friends."

"Oh, *I* wouldn't mind. I *do* think it's sensible. But—well—I don't think Audrey would feel like that about it."

"Nonsense."

"It isn't nonsense. You know, Nevile, Audrey really

was terribly fond of you. . . . I don't think she'd stand
it for a moment."

"You're quite wrong, Kay. Audrey thinks it would
be quite a good thing."

"Audrey—what do you mean, Audrey thinks? How
do you know what Audrey thinks?"

Nevile looked slightly embarrassed. He cleared his
throat a little self-consciously.

"As a matter of fact, I happened to run into her yesterday when I was up in London."

"You never told me."

Nevile said irritably:

"I'm telling you now. It was absolute chance. I was
walking across the Park and there she was coming towards me. You wouldn't want me to run away from her,
would you?"

"No, of course not," said Kay, staring. "Go on."

"I—we—well, we stopped, of course, and then I
turned round and walked with her. I—I felt it was the
least I could do."

"Go on," said Kay.

"And then we sat down on a couple of chairs and
talked. She was very nice—very nice indeed."

"Delightful for you," said Kay.

"And we got talking, you know, about one thing and
another. . . . She was quite natural and normal—and—
and all that."

"Remarkable!" said Kay.

"And she asked how you were—"

"Very kind of her!"

"And we talked about you for a bit. Really, Kay, she
couldn't have been nicer."

"Darling Audrey!"

"And then it sort of came to me—you know—how
nice it would be if—if you two could be friends—if we
could all get together. And it occurred to me that per-

haps we might manage it at Gull's Point this summer. Sort of place it could happen quite naturally."

"*You* thought of that?"

"I—well—yes, of course. It was all my idea."

"You've never said anything to me about having any such idea."

"Well, I only happened to think of it just then."

"I see. Anyway, you suggested it and Audrey thought it was a marvelous brain wave?"

For the first time, something in Kay's manner seemed to penetrate to Nevile's consciousness.

He said:

"Is anything the matter, gorgeous?"

"Oh, no, nothing! Nothing at all! It didn't occur to you or Audrey whether *I* should think it a marvelous idea?"

Nevile stared at her.

"But, Kay, why on earth should *you* mind?"

Kay bit her lip.

Nevile went on:

"You said yourself—only the other day—"

"Oh, don't go into all that again! I was talking about other people—not *us*."

"But that's partly what made me think of it."

"More fool me. Not that I believe that."

Nevile was looking at her with dismay.

"But, Kay, why should you mind? I mean, there's nothing for you to mind about!"

"Isn't there?"

"Well, I mean—any jealousy or that—would be on the other side." He paused, his voice changed. "You see, Kay, you and I treated Audrey damned badly. No, I don't mean that. It was nothing to do with you. *I* treated her very badly. It's no good just saying I couldn't help myself. I feel that if this could come off

I'd feel better about the whole thing. It would make me a lot happier."

Kay said slowly:

"So you haven't been happy?"

"Darling idiot, what do you mean? Of course I've been happy, radiantly happy. But—"

Kay cut in.

"*But*—that's it! There's always been a but in *this* house. Some damned creeping shadow about the place. Audrey's shadow."

Nevile stared at her.

"You mean to say you're jealous of Audrey?" he said.

"I'm not jealous of her. I'm afraid of her. . . . Nevile, you don't know what Audrey's like."

"Not know what she's like when I've been married to her for over eight years?"

"You don't know," Kay repeated, "what Audrey is like."

*April 30th*

"PREPOSTEROUS!" said Lady Tressilian. She drew herself up on her pillow and glared fiercely round the room. "Absolutely preposterous! Nevile must be mad."

"It does seem rather odd," said Mary Aldin.

Lady Tressilian had a striking-looking profile with a slender bridged nose down which, when so inclined, she could look with telling effect. Though she was now over seventy and in frail health, her native vigor of mind was in no way impaired. She had, it is true, long periods of retreat from life and its emotions when she would lie with half-closed eyes, but from these semicomas she would emerge with all her faculties sharpened to the uttermost, and with an incisive tongue. Propped up by pillows in a large bed set across one corner of her room,

she held her court like some French Queen. Mary Aldin,
a distant cousin, lived with her. The two women got on
together excellently. Mary was thirty-six, but had one
of those smooth ageless faces that change little with
passing years. She might have been thirty or forty-five.
She had a good figure, an air of breeding, and dark hair
to which one lock of white across the front gave a touch
of individuality. It was at one time a fashion, but Mary's
white lock of hair was natural and she had had it since
her girlhood.

She looked down now reflectively at Nevile Strange's
letter which Lady Tressilian had handed to her.

"Yes," she said. "It does seem rather odd."

"You can't tell me," said Lady Tressilian, "that this
is Nevile's own idea! Somebody's put it into his head.
Probably that new wife of his."

"Kay. You think it was Kay's idea?"

"It would be quite like her. New and vulgar! If husbands and wives *have* to advertise their difficulties in
public and have recourse to divorce, then they might at
least part decently. The new wife and the old wife
making friends is quite disgusting to my mind. Nobody
has any *standards* nowadays!"

"I suppose it is just the modern way," said Mary.

"It won't happen in my house," said Lady Tressilian.
"I consider I've done all that could be asked of me
having that scarlet-toed creature here at all."

"She is Nevile's wife."

"Exactly. Therefore I felt that Matthew would have
wished it. He was devoted to the boy and always wanted
him to look on this as his home. Since to refuse to
receive his wife would have made an open breach, I
gave way and asked her here. I do *not* like her—she's
quite the wrong wife for Nevile—no background, no
roots!"

"She's quite well born," said Mary placatingly.

"Bad stock!" said Lady Tressilian. "Her father, as I've told you, had to resign from all his clubs after that card business. Luckily he died shortly after. And her mother was notorious on the Riviera. What a bringing up for the girl. Nothing but hotel life—and that mother! Then she meets Nevile on the tennis courts, makes a dead set at him and never rests until she gets him to leave his wife—of whom he was extremely fond—and go off with her! I blame her entirely for the whole thing!"

Mary smiled faintly. Lady Tressilian had the old-fashioned characteristic of always blaming the woman and being indulgent towards the man in the case.

"I suppose, strictly speaking, Nevile was equally to blame," she suggested.

"Nevile was very much to blame," agreed Lady Tressilian. "He had a charming wife who had always been devoted—perhaps too devoted—to him. Nevertheless, if it hadn't been for that girl's persistence, I am convinced he would have come to his senses. But she was determined to marry him! Yes, my sympathies are entirely with Audrey. I am very fond of Audrey."

Mary sighed.

"It has all been very difficult," she said.

"Yes, indeed. One is at a loss to know how to act in such difficult circumstances. Matthew was fond of Audrey, and so am I, and one cannot deny that she was a very good wife to Nevile though perhaps it is a pity that she could not have shared his amusements more. She was never an athletic girl. The whole business was very distressing. When I was a girl, these things simply did not happen. Men had their affairs, naturally, but they were not allowed to break up married life."

"Well, they happen now," said Mary bluntly.

"Exactly. You have so much common sense, dear. It is of no use recalling bygone days. These things happen, and girls like Kay Mortimer steal other women's husbands and nobody thinks the worse of them!"

"Except people like you, Camilla!"

"I don't count. That Kay creature doesn't worry whether I approve of her or not. She's too busy having a good time. Nevile can bring her here when he comes and I'm even willing to receive her friends—though I do not much care for that very theatrical-looking young man who is always hanging round her—what is his name?"

"Ted Latimer?"

"That is it. A friend of her Riviera days—and I should very much like to know how he manages to live as he does."

"By his wits," suggested Mary.

"One might pardon that. I rather fancy he lives by his looks. Not a pleasant friend for Nevile's wife! I disliked the way he came down last summer and stayed at the Easterhead Bay Hotel while they were here."

Mary looked out of the open window. Lady Tressilian's house was situated on a steep cliff overhanging the river Tern. On the other side of the river was the newly created summer resort of Easterhead Bay, consisting of a big sandy bathing beach, a cluster of modern bungalows and a large hotel on the headland looking out to sea. Saltcreek itself was a straggling picturesque fishing village set on the side of a hill. It was old-fashioned, conservative and deeply contemptuous of Easterhead Bay and its summer visitors.

The Easterhead Bay Hotel was nearly exactly opposite Lady Tressilian's house and Mary looked across the narrow strip of water at it now where it stood in its blatant white newness.

"I am glad," said Lady Tressilian, closing her eyes, "that Matthew never saw that vulgar building. The coastline was *quite* unspoilt in his time."

Sir Matthew and Lady Tressilian had come to Gull's Point thirty years ago. It was ten years since Sir Matthew, an enthusiastic sailing man, had capsized his dinghy and been drowned almost in front of his wife's eyes.

Everybody had expected her to sell Gull's Point and leave Saltcreek but Lady Tressilian had not done so. She had lived on in the house, and her only visible reaction had been to dispose of all the boats and do away with the boathouse. There were no boats available for guests at Gull's Point. They had to walk along to the ferry and hire a boat from one of the rival boatmen there.

Mary said, hesitating a little:

"Shall I write, then, to Nevile and tell him that what he proposes does not fit in with your plans?"

"I certainly shall not dream of interfering with Audrey's visit. She has always come to us in September and I shall not ask her to change her plans."

Mary said, looking down at the letter:

"You did see that Nevile says Audrey—er—approves of the idea—that she is quite willing to meet Kay?"

"I simply don't believe it," said Lady Tressilian. "Nevile, like all men, believes what he wants to believe!"

Mary persisted:

"He says he has actually spoken to her about it."

"What a very odd thing to do! No—perhaps, after all, it isn't!"

Mary looked at her inquiringly.

"Like Henry the Eighth," said Lady Tressilian.

Mary looked puzzled.

Lady Tressilian elaborated her last remark.

"Conscience, you know! Henry was always trying to get Catherine to agree that the divorce was the right thing. Nevile knows that he has behaved badly—he wants to feel *comfortable* about it all. So he has been trying to bully Audrey into saying everything is all right and that she'll come and meet Kay and that she doesn't mind at all."

"I wonder," said Mary slowly.

Lady Tressilian looked at her sharply.

"What's in your mind, my dear?"

"I was wondering——" She stopped, then went on: "It —it seems so *unlike* Nevile—this letter! You don't think that, for some reason, Audrey *wants* this—this meeting?"

"Why should she?" said Lady Tressilian sharply. "After Nevile left her she went to her aunt, Mrs. Royde, at the Rectory, and had a complete breakdown. She was absolutely like a ghost of her former self. Obviously it hit her terribly hard. She's one of those quiet, self-contained people who feel things intensely."

Mary moved uneasily.

"Yes, she is intense. A queer girl in many ways . . ."

"She suffered a lot. . . . Then the divorce went through and Nevile married the girl and little by little Audrey began to get over it. Now she's almost back to her old self. You can't tell me she wants to rake up old memories again?"

Mary said with gentle obstinacy:

"Nevile says she does."

The old lady looked at her curiously.

"You're extraordinarily obstinate about this, Mary. Why? Do you *want* to have them here together?"

Mary Aldin flushed.

"No, of course not."

Lady Tressilian said sharply:

"It's not *you* who have been suggesting all this to Nevile?"

"How can you be so absurd?"

"Well, I don't believe for a minute it's really his

idea. It's not *like* Nevile." She paused a minute, then her face cleared. "It's the first of May tomorrow, isn't it? Well, on the third Audrey is coming to stay with the Darlingtons at Esbank. It's only twenty miles away. Write and ask her to come over and lunch here."

*May 5th*

"Mrs. Strange, m'lady."

Audrey Strange came into the big bedroom, crossed the room to the big bed, stooped down and kissed the old lady and sat down in the chair placed ready for her.

"Nice to see you, my dear," said Lady Tressilian.

"And nice to see you," said Audrey.

There was a quality of intangibility about Audrey Strange. She was of medium height with very small hands and feet. Her hair was ash blonde and there was very little color in her face. Her eyes were set wide apart and were a clear, pale grey. Her features were small and regular, a straight little nose set in a small oval pale face. With such coloring, with a face that was pretty but not beautiful, she had nevertheless a quality about her that could not be ignored and that drew your eyes to her again and again. She was a little like a ghost, but you felt at the same time that a ghost might be possessed of more reality than a live human being. . . .

She had a singularly lovely voice; soft and clear like a small silver bell.

For some minutes she and the old lady talked of mutual friends and current events. Then Lady Tressilian said:

"Besides the pleasure of seeing you, my dear, I asked you to come because I've had rather a curious letter from Nevile."

Audrey looked up. Her eyes were wide, tranquil and calm. She said:

"Oh, yes?"

"He suggests—a preposterous suggestion, *I* call it!—that he and—and Kay should come here in September. He says he wants you and Kay to be friends and that you yourself think it a good idea."

She waited. Presently Audrey said in her gentle placid voice:

"Is it—so preposterous?"

"My dear—do you really want this to happen?"

Audrey was silent again for a minute or two, then she said gently:

"I think, you know, it might be rather a good thing."

"You really want to meet this—you want to meet Kay?"

"I do think, Camilla, that it might—simplify things."

"Simplify things!" Lady Tressilian repeated the words helplessly.

Audrey spoke very softly.

"Dear Camilla. You have been so good. If Nevile wants this—"

"A fig for what Nevile wants!" said Lady Tressilian robustly. "Do *you* want it, that's the question?"

A little color came into Audrey's cheeks. It was the soft delicate glow of a sea shell.

"Yes," she said. "I do want it."

"Well," said Lady Tressilian "—well—"

She stopped.

"But, of course," said Audrey. "It is entirely your choice. It is your house and—"

Lady Tressilian shut her eyes.

"I'm an old woman," she said. "Nothing makes sense any more."

"But of course—I'll come some other time—Any time will suit me."

"You'll come in September as you always do," snapped Lady Tressilian. "And Nevile and Kay shall come too. I may be old but I can adapt myself, I suppose, as well as anyone else, to the changing phases of modern life. Not another word, that's settled."

She closed her eyes again. After a minute or two she said, peering through half-shut lids at the young woman sitting beside her:

"Well, got what you want?"

Audrey started.

"Oh, yes, yes. Thank you."

"My dear," said Lady Tressilian, and her voice was deep and concerned, "are you sure this isn't going to hurt you? You were very fond of Nevile, you know. This may reopen old wounds."

Audrey was looking down at her small gloved hands. One of them, Lady Tressilian noticed, was clenched on the side of the bed.

Audrey lifted her head. Her eyes were calm and untroubled.

She said:

"All that is quite over now. *Quite* over."

Lady Tressilian leaned more heavily back on her pillows.

"Well—you should know. I'm tired—you must leave me now, dear. Mary is waiting for you downstairs. Tell them to send Barrett to me."

Barrett was Lady Tressilian's elderly and devoted maid.

She came in to find her mistress lying back with closed eyes.

"The sooner I'm out of this world the better, Barrett," said Lady Tressilian. "I don't understand anything or anyone in it."

"Ah! don't say that, my lady, you're tired."

"Yes, I'm tired. Take that eiderdown off my feet and give me a dose of my tonic."

"It's Mrs. Strange coming that upset you. A nice lady, but *she* could do with a tonic, I'd say. Not healthy. Always looks as though she's seeing things other people don't see. But she's got a lot of character. She makes herself *felt,* as you might say."

"That's very true, Barrett," said Lady Tressilian. "Yes, that's very true."

"And she's not the kind you forget easily, either. I've often wondered if Mr. Nevile thinks about her sometimes. The new Mrs. Strange is very handsome— very handsome indeed—but Miss Audrey is the kind you remember when she isn't there."

Lady Tressilian said with a sudden chuckle:

"Nevile's a fool to want to bring those two women together. *He's* the one who'll be sorry for it!"

## May 29th

THOMAS ROYDE, pipe in mouth, was surveying the progress of his packing with which the deft-fingered Malayan No. 1 boy was busy. Occasionally his glance shifted to the view over the plantations. For some six months he would not see that view which had been so familiar for the past seven years.

It would be queer to be in England again.

Allen Drake, his partner, looked in.

"Hullo, Thomas, how goes it?"

"All set now."

"Come and have a drink, you lucky devil. I'm consumed with envy."

Thomas Royde moved slowly out of the bedroom and joined his friend. He did not speak, for Thomas Royde was a man singularly economical of words. His friends had learned to gauge his reactions correctly from the quality of his silences.

A rather thickset figure, with a straight solemn face and observant thoughtful eyes. He walked a little sideways, crablike. This, the result of being jammed in a door during an earthquake, had contributed towards his nickname of the Hermit Crab. It had left his right arm and shoulder partially helpless which, added to an artificial stiffness of gait, often led people to think he was feeling shy and awkward when in reality he seldom felt anything of the kind.

Allen Drake mixed the drinks.

"Well," he said. "Good hunting!"

Royde said something that sounded like "Ah hum."

Drake looked at him curiously.

"Phlegmatic as ever," he remarked. "Don't know how you manage it. How long is it since you went home?"

"Seven years—nearer eight."

"It's a long time. Wonder you haven't gone completely native."

"Perhaps I have."

"You always did belong to Our Dumb Friends rather than to the human race! Planned out your leave?"

"Well—yes—partly."

The bronze impassive face took a sudden and a deeper brick red tinge.

Allen Drake said with lively astonishment:

"I believe there's a girl! Damn it all, you *are* blushing!"

Thomas Royde said rather huskily:

"Don't be a fool!"

And he drew very hard on his ancient pipe.

He broke all previous records by continuing the conversation himself.

"Daresay," he said, "I shall find things a bit changed."

Allen Drake asked curiously:

"I've always wondered why you chucked going home last time. Right at the last minute, too."

Royde shrugged his shoulders.

"Thought that shooting trip might be interesting. Bad news from home about then."

"Of course. I forgot. Your brother was killed—in that motoring accident."

Thomas Royde nodded.

Drake reflected that, all the same, it seemed a curious reason for putting off a journey home. There was a mother—he believed, a sister also. Surely at such a time— Then he remembered something. Thomas had canceled his passage *before* the news of his brother's death arrived.

Allen looked at his friend curiously. Dark horse, old Thomas?

After a lapse of three years he could ask:

"You and your brother great pals?"

"Adrian and I? Not particularly. Each of us always went his own way. He was a barrister."

"Yes," thought Drake, "a very different life. Chambers in London, parties—a living earned by the shrewd use of the tongue." He reflected that Adrian Royde must have been a very different chap from old Silent Thomas.

"Your mother's alive, isn't she?"

"The Mater? Yes."

"And you've got a sister, too."

Thomas shook his head.

"Oh, I thought you had. In that snapshot—"

Royde mumbled. "Not a sister. Sort of distant cousin or something. Brought up with us because she was an orphan."

Once more a slow tide of color suffused the bronzed skin.

Drake thought, "Hello—o—?"

He said: "Is she married?"

"She was. Married that fellow Nevile Strange."

"Fellow who plays tennis and rackets and all that?"

"Yes. She divorced him."

"And you're going home to try your luck with her," thought Drake.

Mercifully he changed the subject of the conversation.

"Going to get any fishing or shooting?"

"Shall go home first. Then I thought of doing a bit of sailing down at Saltcreek."

"I know it. Attractive little place. Rather a decent old-fashioned hotel there."

"Yes. The Balmoral Court. May stay there, or may put up with friends who've got a house there."

"Sounds all right to me."

"Ah hum. Nice peaceful place, Saltcreek. Nobody to hustle you."

"I know," said Drake. "The kind of place where nothing ever happens.".


*June 16th*


"IT IS REALLY most annoying," said old Mr. Treves. "For twenty-five years now I have been to the Marine Hotel at Leahead—and now, would you believe it, the whole place is being pulled down. Widening the front or some nonsense of that kind. Why they can't let these seaside places alone—Leahead always had a peculiar charm of its own—Regency—pure Regency."

Sir Rufus Lord said consolingly:

"Still, there are other places to stay there, I suppose?"

"I really don't feel I can go to Leahead at all. At the Marine, Mrs. Mackay understood my requirements perfectly. I had the same rooms every year—and there was hardly ever a change in the service. And the cooking was excellent—quite excellent."

"What about trying Saltcreek? There's rather a nice old-fashioned hotel there. The Balmoral Court. Tell you who keeps it. Couple of the name of Rogers. She used to be cook to old Lord Mounthead—he had the best dinners in London. She married the butler and they run this hotel now. It sounds to me just your kind of place. Quiet—none of these jazz bands—and first-class cooking and service."

"It's an idea—it's certainly an idea. Is there a sheltered terrace?"

"Yes—a covered-in verandah and a terrace beyond. You can get sun or shade as you prefer. I can give you some introductions in the neighborhood, too, if you like. There's old Lady Tressilian—she lives almost next door. A charming house and she herself is a delightful woman in spite of being very much of an invalid."

"The judge's widow, do you mean?"

"That's it."

"I used to know Matthew Tressilian, and I think I've met her. A charming woman—though of course that's a long time ago. Saltcreek is near St. Loo, isn't it? I've several friends in that part of the world. Do you know, I really think Saltcreek is a very good idea. I shall write and get particulars. The middle of August is when I wish to go there—the middle of August to the middle of September. There is a garage for the car, I suppose? And my chauffeur?"

"Oh, yes. It's thoroughly up to date."

"Because, as you know, I have to be careful about walking up hill. I should prefer rooms on the ground floor, though I suppose there is a lift."

"Oh, yes, all that sort of thing."

"It sounds," said Mr. Treves, "as though it would solve my problem perfectly. And I should enjoy renewing my acquaintance with Lady Tressilian."

### July 28th

KAY STRANGE, dressed in shorts and a canary-colored woolly, was leaning forward watching the tennis players. It was the semifinal of the tournament, men's singles, and Nevile was playing young Merrick who was regarded as the coming star in the tennis firmament. His brilliance was undeniable—some of his serves quite unreturnable—but he occasionally struck a wild patch when the older man's experience and court craft won the day.

The score was three-all in the final set.

Slipping onto a seat next to Kay, Ted Latimer observed in a lazy, ironic voice:

"Devoted wife watches her husband slash his way to victory!"

Kay started.

"How you startled me. I didn't know you were there."

"I am always there. You should know that by this time."

Ted Latimer was twenty-five and extremely good looking—even though unsympathetic old colonels were wont to say of him:

"Touch of the Dago!"

He was dark and beautifully sunburned and a wonderful dancer.

His dark eyes could be very eloquent, and he managed his voice with the assurance of an actor. Kay had known him since she was fifteen. They had oiled and sunned themselves at Juan-les-Pins, had danced together and played tennis together. They had been not only friends but allies.

Young Merrick was serving from the left hand court. Nevile's return was unplayable, a superb shot to the extreme corner.

"Nevile's backhand is good," said Ted. "It's better than his forehand. Merrick's weak on the backhand and Nevile knows it. He's going to pound at it all he knows how."

The game ended. *"Four-three—Strange leads."*

He took the next game on his service. Young Merrick was hitting out wildly.

*"Five-three."*

"Good for Nevile," said Latimer.

And then the boy pulled himself together. His play became cautious. He varied the pace of his shots.

"He's got a head on him," said Ted. "And his footwork is first class. It's going to be a fight."

Slowly the boy pulled up to five-all. Then went to seven-all and Merrick finally won the match at nine-seven.

Nevile came up to the net, grinning and shaking his head ruefully, to shake hands.

"Youth tells," said Ted Latimer. "Nineteen against thirty-three. But I can tell you the reason, Kay, why Nevile has never been actually championship class. He's too good a loser."

"Nonsense."

"It isn't. Nevile, blast him, is always the complete good sportsman. I've never seen him lose his temper over losing a match."

"Of course not," said Kay. "People don't."

"Oh, yes, they do! We've all seen them. Tennis stars who give way to nerves—and who damn well snatch every advantage. But old Nevile—he's always ready to take the count and grin. Let the best man win and all that. God, how I hate the public-school spirit! Thank the Lord I never went to one."

Kay turned her head.

"Being rather spiteful, aren't you?"

"Positively feline!"

"I wish you wouldn't make it so clear you don't like Nevile."

"Why should I like him? He pinched my girl."

His eyes lingered on her.

"I wasn't your girl. Circumstances forbade."

"Quite so. Not even the proverbial tuppence a year between us."

"Shut up. I fell in love with Nevile and married him——"

"And he's a jolly good fellow——and so say all of us!"

"Are you trying to annoy me?"

She turned her head as she asked the question. He smiled——and presently she returned his smile.

"How's the summer going, Kay?"

"So, so. Lovely yachting trip. I'm rather tired of all this tennis business."

"How long have you got of it? Another month?"

"Yes. Then in September we go to Gull's Point for a fortnight."

"I shall be at the Easterhead Bay Hotel," said Ted. "I've booked my room."

"It's going to be a lovely party!" said Kay. "Nevile and I, and Nevile's Ex, and some Malayan planter who's home on leave."

"That does sound hilarious!"

"And the dowdy cousin, of course. Slaving away around that unpleasant old woman——and she won't get anything for it, either, since the money comes to me and Nevile."

"Perhaps," said Ted, "she doesn't know that?"

"That would be rather funny," said Kay.

But she spoke absently.

She stared down at the racket she was twiddling in her hands. She caught her breath suddenly.

"Oh, Ted!"

"What's the matter, sugar?"

"I don't know. It's just sometimes I get—I get cold feet! I get scared and feel queer."

"That doesn't sound like you, Kay."

"It doesn't, does it? Anyway," she smiled rather uncertainly, "you'll be at the Easterhead Bay Hotel."

"All according to plan."

When Kay met Nevile outside the changing rooms, he said:

"I see the boy friend's arrived."

"Ted?"

"Yes, the faithful dog—or faithful lizard might be more apt."

"You don't like him, do you?"

"Oh, I don't mind him. If it amuses you to pull him around on a string—"

He shrugged his shoulders.

Kay said:

"I believe you're jealous."

"Of Latimer?" His surprise was genuine.

Kay said:

"Ted's supposed to be very attractive."

"I'm sure he is. He has that lithe South American charm."

"You *are* jealous."

Nevile gave her arm a friendly squeeze.

"No, I'm not, gorgeous. You can have your tame adorers—a whole court of them if you like. I'm the man in possession and possession is nine points of the law."

"You've very sure of yourself," said Kay with a slight pout.

"Of course. You and I are Fate. Fate let us meet.

Fate brought us together. Do you remember when we met at Cannes and I was going on to Estoril and suddenly, when I got there, the first person I saw was lovely Kay! I knew then that it was Fate—and that I couldn't escape."

"It wasn't exactly Fate," said Kay. "It was me!"

"What do you mean by 'it was me'?"

"Because it was! You see, I heard you say in the hotel you were going to Estoril, so I set to work on Mums and got her all worked up—and that's why the first person you saw when you got there was Kay."

Nevile looked at her with a rather curious expression. He said slowly: "You never told me that before."

"No, because it wouldn't have been good for you. It might have made you conceited! But I always *have* been good at planning. Things don't happen unless you make them! You call me a nitwit sometimes—but in my own way I'm quite clever. I make things happen. Sometimes I have to plan a long way beforehand."

"The brainwork must be intense."

"It's all very well to laugh."

Nevile said with a sudden curious bitterness, "Am I just beginning to understand the woman I've married? For Fate—read Kay!"

Kay said:

"You're not cross, are you, Nevile?"

He said rather absently:

"No—no, of course not. I was just—thinking. . . ."

*August 10th*

"AND BANG goes my holiday," said Superintendent Battle disgustedly.

Mrs. Battle was disappointed, but long years as the

wife of a police officer had prepared her to take disappointments philosophically.

"Oh, well," she said, "it can't be helped. And I suppose it *is* an interesting case?"

"Not so that you'd notice it," said Superintendent Battle. "It's got the Foreign Officer in a twitter—all those tall, thin young men rushing about and saying Hush Hush here, there and everywhere. It'll straighten out easy enough—and we shall save everybody's face. But it's not the kind of case I'd put in my Memoirs, supposing I was ever foolish enough to write any."

"We could put our holiday off, I suppose—" began Mrs. Battle doubtfully but her husband interrupted her decisively.

"Not a bit of it. You and the girls go off to Britlington —the rooms have been booked since March—pity to waste them. I tell you what I'll do—go down and spend a week with Jim when this blows over."

Jim was Superintendent Battle's nephew, Inspector James Leach.

"Saltington's quite close to Easterhead Bay and Saltcreek," he went on. "I can get a bit of sea air and a dip in the briny."

Mrs. Battle sniffed.

"More likely he'll rope you in to help him over a case!"

"They don't have any cases this time of the year—unless it's a woman who pinches a few sixpennyworths from Woolworth's. And anyway Jim's all right—he doesn't need his wits sharpened for him."

"Oh, well," said Mrs. Battle. "I suppose it will work out all right but it is disappointing."

"These things are sent to try us," Superintendent Battle assured her.

# SNOW WHITE AND ROSE RED

## 1

THOMAS ROYDE found Mary Aldin waiting for him on the platform at Saltington when he got out of the train.

He had only a dim recollection of her and now that he saw her again, he was rather surprisedly aware of pleasure at her brisk capable way of dealing with things.

She called him by his Christian name.

"How nice to see you, Thomas. After all these years."

"Nice of you to put me up. Hope it isn't a bother."

"Not at all. On the contrary. You'll be particularly welcome. Is that your porter? Tell him to bring the things out this way. I've got the car right at the end."

The bags were stowed in the Ford. Mary took the wheel and Royde got in beside her. They drove off and Thomas noticed that she was a good driver, deft and careful in traffic and with a nice judgment of distance and spaces.

Saltington was seven miles from Saltcreek. Once they were out of the small market town and on the open road, Mary Aldin reopened the subject of his visit.

"Really, Thomas, your visit just now is going to be a godsend. Things are rather difficult—and a stranger— or rather an outsider is just what is needed."

"What's the trouble?"

His manner, as always, was incurious—almost lazy. He asked the question, it seemed, more from politeness than because he had any desire for the information. It was a manner particularly soothing to Mary Aldin. She wanted badly to talk to someone—but she much preferred to talk to someone who was not too much interested.

She said:

"Well—we've got rather a difficult situation. Audrey is here, as you probably know?"

She paused questioningly and Thomas Royde nodded.

"And Nevile and his wife too."

Thomas Royde's eyebrows went up. He said after a minute or two:

"Bit awkward—what?"

"Yes, it is. It was all Nevile's idea."

She paused. Royde did not speak, but as though aware of some current of disbelief issuing from him, she repeated assertively:

"It *was* Nevile's idea."

"Why?"

She raised her hands for a moment from the steering wheel.

"Oh, some modern reaction! All sensible and friends together. That idea. But I don't think, you know, it's working very well."

"Possibly it mightn't." He added, "What's the new wife like?"

"Kay? Good looking, of course. Really very good looking. And quite young."

"And Nevile's keen on her?"

"Oh, yes. Of course they've only been married a year and a half."

Thomas Royde turned his head slowly to look at her. His mouth smiled a little. Mary said hastily:

"I didn't mean that exactly."

"Come now, Mary. I think you did."

"Well, one can't help seeing that they've really got very little in common. Their friends, for instance—" She came to a stop.

Royde asked:

"He met her, didn't he, on the Riviera? I don't know much about it. Only just the bare facts that the Mater wrote."

"Yes, they met first at Cannes. Nevile was attracted but I should imagine he'd been attracted before—in a harmless sort of way. I still think myself that if he'd been left to himself nothing would have come of it. He *was* fond of Audrey, you know?"

Thomas nodded.

Mary went on:

"I don't think he wanted to break up his marriage— I'm sure he didn't. But the girl was absolutely determined. She wouldn't rest until she'd got him to leave his wife—and what's a man to do under those circumstances? It flatters him, of course."

"Head over ears in love with him, was she?"

"I suppose it may have been that."

Mary's tone sounded doubtful. She met his inquiring glance with a flush.

"What a cat I am! There's a young man always hanging about—good looking in a gigolo kind of way—an

old friend of hers—and I can't help wondering sometimes whether the fact that Nevile is very well off and
distinguished and all that didn't have something to do
with it. The girl hadn't a penny of her own, I gather."

She paused, looking rather ashamed. Thomas Royde
merely said: "Um-hum," in a speculative voice.

"However," said Mary, "that's probably plain cat!
The girl is what one would call glamorous—and that
probably rouses the feline instincts of middle-aged
spinsters."

Royde looked thoughtfully at her, but his poker face
showed no recognizable reaction. He said, after a
minute or two:

"What, exactly, is the present trouble about?"

"Really, you know, I haven't the least idea! That's
what's so odd. Naturally we consulted Audrey first—
and she seemed to have no feeling against meeting
Kay—she was charming about it all. She *has* been
charming. No one could have been nicer. Audrey, of
course, in everything she does is always just right. Her
manner to them both is perfect. She's very reserved, as
you know, and one never has any idea of what she is
really thinking or feeling—but honestly I don't believe
she minds *at all*."

"No reason why she should," said Thomas Royde.
He added rather belatedly, "After all, it's three years
ago."

"Do people like Audrey forget? She was very fond of
Nevile."

Thomas Royde shifted in his seat.

"She's only thirty-two. Got her life in front of her."

"Oh, I know. But she *did* take it hard. She had
quite a bad nervous breakdown, you know."

"I know. The Mater wrote me."

"In a way," said Mary, "I think it was good for your
mother to have Audrey to look after. It took her mind

off her own grief—about your brother's death. We were so sorry about that."

"Yes. Poor old Adrian. Always did drive too fast."

There was a pause. Mary stretched out her hand as a sign she was taking the turn that led down the hill to Saltcreek.

Presently, as they were slipping down the narrow twisting road, she said:

"Thomas—you know Audrey very well?"

"So, so. Haven't seen much of her for the last ten years."

"No, but you knew her as a child. She was like a sister to you and Adrian?"

He nodded.

"Was she—was she at all unbalanced in any way? Oh, I don't mean that quite the way it sounds. But I've a feeling that there is something very wrong with her now. She's so completely detached, her poise is so unnaturally perfect—but I wonder sometimes what is going on behind the façade. I've a feeling, now and then, of some really powerful emotion. And I don't quite know what it is! But I do feel that she isn't *normal*. There's *something!* It worries me. I do know that there's an atmosphere in the house that affects everybody. We're all nervous and jumpy. But I don't know what it is. And sometimes, Thomas, it frightens me."

"Frightens you?" His slow wondering tone made her pull herself together with a little nervous laugh.

"It does sound absurd. . . . But that's what I meant just now—your arrival will be good for us—create a diversion. Ah, here we are."

They had slipped round the last corner. Gull's Point was built on a plateau of rock overlooking the river. On two sides it had sheer cliff going down to the water. The gardens and tennis court were on the left of the house. The garage—a modern afterthought—was actually further along the road, on the other side of it.

Mary said:

"I'll put the car away now and come back. Hurstall will look after you."

Hurstall, the aged butler, was greeting Thomas with the pleasure of an old friend.

"Very glad to see you, Mr. Royde, after all these years. And so will her ladyship be. You're in the East Room, sir. I think you'll find everyone in the garden, unless you want to go to your room first."

Thomas shook his head. He went through the drawing room and up to the window which opened onto the terrace. He stood there a moment, watching, unobserved himself.

Two women were the only occupants of the terrace. One was sitting on the corner of the balustrade looking out over the water. The other woman was watching her.

The first was Audrey—the other, he knew, must be Kay Strange. Kay did not know she was being looked over and she took no pains to disguise her expression. Thomas Royde was not, perhaps, a very observant man where women were concerned, but he could not fail to notice that Kay Strange disliked Audrey Strange very much.

As for Audrey, she was looking out across the river and seemed unconscious of, or indifferent to, the other's presence.

It was over seven years since Thomas had seen Audrey Strange. He studied her now very carefully. Had she changed, and, if so, in what way?

There was a change, he decided. She was thinner, paler, altogether more ethereal looking—but there was something else, something he could not quite define. It was as though she were holding herself tightly in leash, watching over every movement—and yet all the time intensely aware of everything going on round her. She was like a person, he thought, who had a secret to hide. But what secret? He knew a little of the events that had befallen her in the last few years. He had been prepared for lines of sorrow and loss—but this was something else. She was like a child who, by a tightly clenched hand over a treasure, calls attention to what it wants to hide.

And then his eyes went to the other woman—the girl who was now Nevile Strange's wife. Beautiful, yes. Mary Aldin had been right. He rather fancied dangerous, too. He thought: I wouldn't like to thrust her near Audrey if she had a knife in her hand. . . .

And yet why should she hate Nevile's first wife? All that was over and done with. Audrey had no part or parcel in their lives nowadays.

Footsteps rang out on the terrace, as Nevile came round the corner of the house. He looked warm and was carrying a picture paper.

"Here's the *Illustrated Review*," he said. "Couldn't get the other—"

Then two things happened at precisely the same minute.

Kay said: "Oh, good, give it to me," and Audrey, without moving her head, held out her hand almost absentmindedly.

Nevile had stopped halfway between the two women. A dawn of embarrassment showed in his face. Before he could speak, Kay said, her voice rising with a slight note of hysteria:

"I want it. Give it to me! Give it to me, Nevile!"

Audrey Strange started, turned her head, withdrew her hand and murmured with just the slightest air of confusion:

"Oh, sorry. I thought you were speaking to me, Nevile."

Thomas Royde saw the color come up brick red in
Nevile Strange's neck. He took three quick steps forward
and held out the picture paper to Audrey.

She said, hesitating, her air of embarrassment growing:

"Oh, but—"

Kay pushed back her chair with a rough movement.
She stood up, then, turning, she made for the drawing-
room window. Royde had no time to move before she
had charged into him blindly.

The shock made her recoil; she looked at him as he
apologized. He saw then why she had not seen him, her
eyes were brimming with tears—tears, he fancied, of
anger.

"Hullo," she said. "Who are you? Oh! of course, the
man from Malay!"

"Yes," said Thomas. "I'm the man from Malay."

"I wish to God I was in Malay," said Kay. "Anywhere but here! I loathe this beastly lousy house! I
loathe everyone in it!"

Emotional scenes always alarmed Thomas. He regarded Kay warily and murmured nervously:

"Ah-hum."

"Unless they're careful," said Kay, "I shall kill
someone! Either Nevile or that whey-faced cat out
there!"

She brushed past him and went out of the room bang-
ing the door.

Thomas Royde stood stock still. He was not quite
sure what to do next, but he was glad that young Mrs.
Strange had gone. He stood and looked at the door that
she had slammed so vigorously. Something of a tiger
cat, the new Mrs. Strange.

The window was darkened as Nevile Strange paused
in the space between the French doors. He was breathing rather fast.

He greeted Thomas vaguely.

"Oh—er—hullo, Royde, didn't know you'd arrived. I say, have you seen my wife?"

"She passed through about a minute ago," said the other.

Nevile in his turn went out through the drawing-room door. He was looking annoyed.

Thomas Royde went slowly through the open window. He was not a heavy walker. Not until he was a couple of yards away, did Audrey turn her head.

Then he saw those wide-apart eyes open, saw her lips part. She slipped down from the wall and came towards him, hands outstretched.

"Oh, Thomas," she said. "Dear Thomas! How glad I am you've come."

As he took the two small white hands in his and bent down to her, Mary Aldin in her turn arrived at the French windows. Seeing the two on the terrace she checked herself, watched them for a moment or two, then slowly turned away and went back into the house.

## II

UPSTAIRS, NEVILE had found Kay in her bedroom. The only large double bedroom in the house was Lady Tressilian's. A married couple were always given the two rooms with communicating door and a small bath-room beyond on the west side of the house. It was a small isolated suite.

Nevile passed through his own room and on into his wife's. Kay had flung herself down on her bed. Raising a tear-stained face, she cried out angrily:

"So you've come! About time, too!"

"What *is* all this fuss about? Have you gone quite crazy, Kay?"

Nevile spoke quietly, but there was a dint at the corner of his nostril that registered restrained anger.

"Why did you give that *Illustrated Review* to her and not to me?"

"Really, Kay, you are a child! All this fuss about a wretched little picture paper."

"You gave it to her and not to me," repeated Kay obstinately.

"Well, why not? What does it matter?"

"It matters to me."

"I don't know what's wrong with you. You can't behave in this hysterical fashion when you're staying in other people's houses. Don't you know how to behave in public?"

"Why did you give it to Audrey?"

"Because she wanted it."

"So did I, and I'm your wife."

"All the more reason, in that case, for giving it to an older woman and one who, technically, is no relation."

"She scored off me! She wanted to and she did. You were on her side!"

"You're talking like an idiotic jealous child. For goodness' sake, control yourself, and try and behave properly in public!"

"Like she does, I suppose?"

Nevile said coldly:

"At any rate Audrey can behave like a lady. She doesn't make an exhibition of herself."

"She's turning you against me! She hates me and she's getting her revenge."

"Look here, Kay, will you stop being melodramatic and completely foolish? I'm fed up!"

"Then let's go away from here! Let's go tomorrow. I hate this place!"

"We've only been here four days."

"It's quite enough! Do let's go, Nevile."

"Now look here, Kay, I've had enough of this. We came here for a fortnight and I'm going to stay for a fortnight."

"If you do," said Kay, "you'll be sorry. You and your Audrey! You think she's wonderful!"

"I don't think Audrey is wonderful. I think she's an extremely nice and kindly person whom I've treated very badly and who has been most generous and forgiving."

"That's where you're wrong," said Kay. She got up from the bed. Her fury had died down. She spoke seriously—almost soberly.

"Audrey hasn't forgiven you, Nevile. Once or twice I've seen her looking at you. . . . I don't know what is going on in her mind but something is— She's the kind that doesn't let anyone know what they're thinking."

"It's a pity," said Nevile, "that there aren't more people like that."

Kay's face went very white.

"Do you mean that for me?" There was a dangerous edge to her voice.

"Well—you haven't shown much reticence, have you? Every bit of ill temper and spite that comes into your mind you blurt straight out. You make a fool of yourself and you make a fool of me!"

"Anything more to say?"

Her voice was icy.

He said in an equally cold tone:

"I'm sorry if you think that was unfair. But it's the plain truth. You've no more self-control than a child."

"You never lose your temper, do you? Always the self-controlled charming-mannered little pukka sahib! I don't believe you've got any feelings. You're just a *fish*—a damned cold-blooded *fish!* Why don't you let yourself go now and then? Why don't you shout at me, swear at me, tell me to go to hell?"

Nevile sighed. His shoulders sagged.

"Oh, Lord," he said.

Turning on his heel he left the room.

### III

"YOU LOOK exactly as you did at seventeen, Thomas Royde," said Lady Tressilian. "Just the same owlish look. And no more conversation now than you had then. Why not?"

Thomas said vaguely:

"I dunno. Never had the gift of the gab."

"Not like Adrian. Adrian was a very clever and witty talker."

"Perhaps that's why. Always left the talking to him."

"Poor Adrian. So much promise."

Thomas nodded.

Lady Tressilian changed her subject. She was granting an audience to Thomas. She usually preferred her visitors one at a time. It did not tire her and she was able to concentrate her attention on them.

"You've been here twenty-four hours," she said. "What do you think of our Situation?"

"Situation?"

"Don't look stupid. You do that deliberately. You know quite well what I mean. The eternal triangle which has established itself under my roof."

Thomas said cautiously:

"Seems a bit of friction."

Lady Tressilian smiled rather diabolically.

"I will confess to you, Thomas, I am rather enjoying myself. This came about through no wish of mine—indeed I did my utmost to prevent it. Nevile was obsti-

nate. He would insist on bringing these two together—
and now he is reaping what he has sown!"

Thomas Royde shifted a little in his chair.

"Seems funny," he said.

"Elucidate," snapped Lady Tressilian.

"Shouldn't have thought Strange was that kind of
chap."

"It's interesting your saying that. Because it is what
I felt. It was uncharacteristic of Nevile. Nevile, like
most men, is usually anxious to avoid any kind of embarrassment or possible unpleasantness. I suspected that
it wasn't originally Nevile's idea—but, if not, I don't
see whose idea it can have been." She paused and said
with only the slightest upward inflection, "It wouldn't
be Audrey's?"

Thomas said promptly, "No, not Audrey."

"And I can hardly believe it was that unfortunate
young woman, Kay's, idea. Not unless she is a really
remarkable actress. You know, I have almost felt
sorry for her lately."

"You don't like her much, do you?"

"No. She seems to me empty-headed and lacking in
any kind of poise. But as I say, I do begin to feel sorry
for her. She is blundering about like a daddy long-legs
in lamplight. She has no idea of what weapons to use.
Bad temper, bad manners, childish rudeness—all things
which have a most unfortunate effect upon a man like
Nevile."

Thomas said quietly:

"I think Audrey is the one who is in a difficult position."

Lady Tressilian gave him a sharp glance.

"You've always been in love with Audrey, haven't
you, Thomas?"

His reply was quite imperturbable.

"Suppose I have."

"Practically from the time you were children to-gether?"

He nodded.

"And then Nevile came along and carried her off from under your nose?"

He moved uneasily in his chair.

"Oh, well—I always knew I hadn't a chance."

"Defeatist," said Lady Tressilian.

"I always have been a dull dog."

"Dobbin!"

"Good old Thomas!—that's what Audrey feels about me."

" 'True Thomas,' " said Lady Tressilian. "That was your nickname, wasn't it?"

He smiled as the words brought back memories of childish days.

"Funny! I haven't heard that for years."

"It might stand you in good stead now," said Lady Tressilian.

She met his glance clearly and deliberately.

"Fidelity," she said, "is a quality that anyone who has been through Audrey's experience might appreciate. The doglike devotion of a lifetime, Thomas, does some-times get its reward."

Thomas Royde looked down, his fingers fumbled with a pipe.

"That," he said, "is what I came home hoping."

*IV*

"So HERE we all are," said Mary Aldin.

Hurstall, the old butler, wiped his forehead. When he went into the kitchen, Mrs. Spicer, the cook, re-marked upon his expression.

"I don't think I can be well and that's the truth," said

Hurstall. "If I can so express myself, everything that's said and done in this house lately seems to me to mean something that's different from what it sounds like—if you know what I mean?"

Mrs. Spicer did not seem to know what he meant, so Hurstall went on:

"Miss Aldin, now, as they all sat down to dinner—she says, *'So here we all are'*—and just that gave me a turn! Made me think of a trainer who's got a lot of wild animals into a cage, and then the cage door shuts. I felt, all of a sudden, as though we were all caught in a trap."

"Law, Mr. Hurstall," said Mrs. Spicer. "You must have eaten something that's disagreed."

"It's not my digestion. It's the way everyone's strung up. The front door banged just now and Mrs. Strange—our Mrs. Strange, Miss Audrey—she jumped as though she had been shot. And there's the silences, too. Very queer they are. It's as though, all of a sudden, everybody's afraid to speak. And then they all break out at once just saying the things that first come into their heads."

"Enough to make anyone embarrassed," said Mrs. Spicer. "Two Mrs. Stranges in the house. What I feel is, it isn't *decent.*"

In the dining room, one of those silences that Hurstall had described was proceeding.

It was with quite an effort that Mary Aldin turned to Kay and said:

"I asked your friend, Mr. Latimer, to dine tomorrow night!"

"Oh, good," said Kay.

Nevile said:

"Latimer? Is he down here?"

"He's staying at the Easterhead Bay Hotel," said Kay.

Nevile said:

"We might go over and dine there one night. How late does the ferry go?"

"Until half past one," said Mary.

"I suppose they dance there in the evenings?"

"Most of the people are about a hundred," said Kay.

"Not very amusing for your friend," said Nevile to Kay.

Mary said quickly:

"We might go over and bathe one day at Easterhead Bay. It's quite warm still and it's a lovely sandy beach."

Thomas Royde said in a low voice to Audrey:

"I thought of going out sailing tomorrow. Will you come?"

"I'd like to."

"We might all go sailing," said Nevile.

"I thought you said you were going to play golf," said Kay.

"I did think of going over to the links. I was right off my wooden shots the other day."

"What a tragedy!" said Kay.

Nevile said good humoredly:

"Golf's a tragic game."

Mary asked Kay if she played.

"Yes—after a fashion."

Nevile said:

"Kay would be very good if she took a little trouble. She's got a natural swing."

Kay said to Audrey:

"You don't play any games, do you?"

"Not really. I play tennis after a fashion—but I'm a complete rabbit."

"Do you still play the piano, Audrey?" asked Thomas. She shook her head.

"Not nowadays."

"You used to play rather well," said Nevile.

"I thought you didn't like music, Nevile," said Kay.

"I don't know much about it," said Nevile vaguely. "I always wondered how Audrey managed to stretch an octave, her hands are so small."

He was looking at them as she laid down her dessert knife and fork.

She flushed a little and said quickly:

"I've got a very long little finger. I expect that helps."

"You must be selfish then," said Kay. "If you're unselfish you have a short little finger."

"Is that true?" asked Mary Aldin. "Then I must be unselfish. Look, my little fingers are quite short."

"I think you are very unselfish," said Thomas Royde, eyeing her thoughtfully.

She went red—and continued, quickly:

"Who's the most unselfish of us? Let's compare little fingers. Mine are shorter than yours, Kay. But Thomas, I think, beats me."

"I beat you both," said Nevile. "Look," he stretched out a hand.

"Only one hand, though," said Kay. "Your left hand little finger is short but your right hand one is much longer. And your left hand is what you are born with and the right hand is what you make of your life. So that means that you were born unselfish but have become much more selfish as time goes on."

"Can you tell fortunes, Kay?" asked Mary Aldin. She stretched out her hand, palm upwards. "A fortune teller told me I should have two husbands and three children. I shall have to hurry up!"

Kay said:

"Those little crosses aren't children, they're journeys. That means you'll take three journeys across water."

"That seems unlikely, too," said Mary Alden.

Thomas Royde asked her:

"Have you traveled much?"

"No, hardly at all."

He heard an undercurrent of regret in her voice.

"You would like to?"

"Above everything."

He thought in his slow reflective way of her life. Always in attendance on an old woman. Calm, tactful, an excellent manager. He asked curiously:

"Have you lived with Lady Tressilian long?"

"For nearly fifteen years. I came to be with her after my father died. He had been a helpless invalid for some years before his death."

And then, answering the question she felt to be in his mind:

"I'm thirty-six. That's what you wanted to know, wasn't it?"

"I did wonder," he admitted. "You might be—any age, you see."

"That's rather a two-edged remark!"

"I suppose it is. I didn't mean it that way."

That somber thoughtful gaze of his did not leave her face. She did not find it embarrassing. It was too free from self-consciousness for that—a genuine thoughtful interest. Seeing his eyes on her hair, she put her hand to the one white lock.

"I've had that," she said, "since I was very young."

"I like it," said Thomas Royde simply.

He went on looking at her. She said at last, in a slightly amused tone of voice, "Well, what is the verdict?"

He reddened under his tan.

"Oh, I suppose it is rude of me to stare. I was wondering about you—what you are really like."

"Please," she said hurriedly and rose from the table. She said as she went into the drawing room with her arm through Audrey's:

"Old Mr. Treves is coming to dinner tomorrow, too."

"Who's he?" asked Nevile.

"He brought an introduction from the Rufus Lords. A delightful old gentleman. He's staying at the Balmoral Court. He's got a weak heart and looks very frail, but his faculties are perfect and he has known a lot of interesting people. He was a solicitor or a barrister—I forget which."

"Everybody down here is terribly old," said Kay discontentedly.

She was standing just under a tall lamp. Thomas was looking that way, and he gave her that same slow interested attention that he gave to anything that was immediately occupying his line of vision.

He was struck suddenly with her intense and passionate beauty. A beauty of vivid coloring, of abundant and triumphant vitality. He looked across from her to Audrey, pale and mothlike in a silvery grey dress.

He smiled to himself and murmured:

"Rose Red and Snow White."

"What?" It was Mary Aldin at his elbow.

He repeated the words. "Like the old fairy story, you know—"

Mary Aldin said:

"It's a very good description. . . ."

## V

MR. TREVES sipped his glass of port appreciatively. A very nice wine. And an excellently cooked and served dinner. Clearly Lady Tressilian had no difficulties with her servants.

The house was well managed, too, in spite of the mistress of it being an invalid.

A pity, perhaps, that the ladies did not leave the dining room when the port went round. He preferred the old-fashioned routine— But these young people had their own ways.

His eyes rested thoughtfully on that brilliant and beautiful young woman who was the wife of Nevile Strange.

It was Kay's night tonight. Her vivid beauty glowed and shone in the candlelit room. Beside her, Ted Latimer's sleek dark head bent to hers. He was playing up to her. She felt triumphant and sure of herself.

The mere sight of such radiant vitality warmed Mr. Treves' old bones.

Youth—there was really nothing like youth!

No wonder the husband had lost his head and left his first wife. Audrey was sitting next to him. A charming creature and a lady—but then that was the kind of woman who invariably did get left, in Mr. Treves' experience.

He glanced at her. Her head had been down and she was staring at her plate. Something in the complete immobility of her attitude struck Mr. Treves. He looked at her more keenly. He wondered what she was thinking about. Charming the way the hair sprang up from that small shell-like ear. . . .

With a little start, Mr. Treves came to himself as he realized that a move was being made. He got hurriedly to his feet.

In the drawing room, Kay Strange went straight to the gramophone and put on a record of dance music.

Mary Aldin said apologetically to Mr. Treves:

"I'm sure you hate jazz."

"Not at all," said Mr. Treves untruly but politely.

"Later, perhaps, we might have some bridge?" she suggested. "But it is no good starting a rubber now, as I know Lady Tressilian is looking forward to having a chat with you."

"That will be delightful. Lady Tressilian never joins you down here?"

"No, she used to come down in an invalid chair. That is why we had a lift put in. But nowadays she prefers her own room. There she can talk to whomsoever she likes, summoning them by a kind of Royal Command."

"Very aptly put, Miss Aldin. I am always sensible of the royal touch in Lady Tressilian's manner."

In the middle of the room, Kay was moving in a slow dance step.

She said:

"Just take that table out of the way, Nevile."

Her voice was autocratic, assured. Her eyes were shining, her lips parted.

Nevile obediently moved the table. Then he took a step towards her, but she turned deliberately towards Ted Latimer.

"Come on, Ted, let's dance."

Ted's arm went round her immediately. They danced, swaying, bending, their steps perfectly together. It was a lovely performance to watch.

Mr. Treves murmured:

"Er—quite professional."

Mary Aldin winced slightly at the word—yet surely Mr. Treves had spoken in simple admiration. She looked at his little wise nut-cracker face. It bore, she thought, an absent-minded look as though he were following some train of thought of his own.

Nevile stood hesitating a minute, then he walked to where Audrey was standing by the window.

"Dance, Audrey?"

His tone was formal, almost cold. Mere politeness, you might have said, inspired his request. Audrey Strange hesitated a minute before nodding her head and taking a step towards him.

Mary Aldin made some commonplace remarks to which Mr. Treves did not reply. He had so far shown no signs of deafness and his courtesy was punctilious—she realized that it was absorption that held him aloof. She could not quite make out if he was watching the dancers, or was staring across the room at Thomas Royde standing alone at the other end.

With a little start Mr. Treves said:

"Excuse me, my dear lady, you were saying?"

"Nothing. Only that it was an unusually fine September."

"Yes, indeed—rain is badly needed locally, so they tell me at my hotel."

"You are comfortable there, I hope?"

"Oh, yes, though I must say I was vexed when I arrived to find—"

Mr. Treves broke off.

Audrey had disengaged herself from Nevile. She said with an apologetic little laugh:

"It's really too hot to dance."

She went towards the open window and out onto the terrace.

"Oh! go after her, you fool," murmured Mary. She meant the remark to be under her breath, but it was loud enough for Mr. Treves to turn and stare at her in astonishment.

She reddened and gave an embarrassed laugh.

"I'm speaking my thoughts aloud," she said ruefully. "But really he does irritate me so. He's so *slow*."

"Mr. Strange?"

"Oh, no, not Nevile. Thomas Royde."

Thomas Royde was just preparing to move forward, but by now Nevile, after a moment's pause, had followed Audrey out of the window.

For a moment Mr. Treves' eye, interestedly speculative, rested on the window, then his attention returned to the dancers.

"A beautiful dancer, young Mr.—Latimer, did you say the name was?"

"Yes, Edward Latimer."

"Ah, yes, Edward Latimer. An old friend, I gather, of Mrs. Strange?"

"Yes."

"And what does this very—er—decorative young gentleman do for a living?"

"Well, really, I don't quite know."

"In-deed," said Mr. Treves, managing to put a good deal of comprehension into one harmless word.

Mary went on:

"He is staying at the Easterhead Bay Hotel."

"A very pleasant situation," said Mr. Treves.

He added dreamily after a moment or two: "Rather an interesting-shaped head—a curious angle from the crown to the neck—rendered less noticeable by the way he has his hair cut, but distinctly unusual." After another pause, he went on, still more dreamily: "The last man I saw with a head like that got ten years' penal servitude for a brutal assault on an elderly jeweler."

"Surely," exclaimed Mary, "you don't mean—"

"Not at all, not at all," said Mr. Treves. "You mistake me entirely. I am suggesting no disparagement of a guest of yours. I was merely pointing out that a hardened and brutal criminal can be in appearance a most charming and personable young man. Odd, but so it is."

He smiled gently at her. Mary said: "You know, Mr. Treves, I think I am a little frightened of you."

"Nonsense, dear lady."

"But I am. You are—such a very shrewd observer."

"My eyes," said Mr. Treves complacently, "are as good as ever they were." He paused and added: "Whether that is fortunate or unfortunate, I cannot at the moment decide."

"How could it be unfortunate?"

Mr. Treves shook his head doubtfully.

"One is sometimes placed in a position of responsibility. The right course of action is not always easy to determine."

Hurstall entered bearing the coffee tray.

After taking it to Mary and the old lawyer, he went down the room to Thomas Royde. Then, by Mary's directions, he put the tray down on a low table and left the room.

Kay called over Ted's shoulder, "We'll finish out this tune."

Mary said: "I'll take Audrey's out to her."

She went to the French windows, cup in hand. Mr. Treves accompanied her. As she paused on the threshold he looked out over her shoulder.

Audrey was sitting on the corner of the balustrade. In the bright moonlight, her beauty came to life—a beauty born of line rather than color. The exquisite line from jaw to ear, the tender modeling of chin and mouth, and the really lovely bones of the head and the small straight nose. That beauty would be there when Audrey Strange was an old woman—it had nothing to do with the covering flesh—it was the bones themselves that were beautiful. The sequined dress she wore accentuated the effect of the moonlight. She sat very still and Nevile Strange stood and looked at her.

Nevile took a step towards her:

"Audrey," he said, "you—"

She shifted her position, then sprang lightly to her feet and clapped a hand to her ear:

"Oh! My earring—I must have dropped it."

"Where? Let me look—"

They both bent down, awkward and embarrassed—and collided in doing so. Audrey sprang away, and Nevile exclaimed:

"Wait a sec—my cuff button—it's caught in your hair. Stand still."

She stood quite still as he fumbled with the button.

"Oo—you're pulling it out by the roots—how clumsy you are, Nevile, do be quick."

"Sorry I—I seem to be all thumbs."

The moonlight was bright enough for the two on-lookers to see what Audrey could not see, the trembling of Nevile's hands as he strove to free the strand of fair silvery hair.

But Audrey herself was trembling too—as though suddenly cold.

Mary Aldin jumped as a quiet voice said behind her:

"Excuse me—"

Thomas Royde passed between them and out.

"Shall I do that, Strange?" he asked.

Nevile straightened up and he and Audrey moved apart.

"It's all right. I've done it."

Nevile's face was rather white.

"You're cold," said Thomas to Audrey. "Come in and have coffee."

She came back with him and Nevile turned away staring out to sea.

"I was bringing it out to you," said Mary. "But perhaps you'd better come in."

"Yes," said Audrey. "I think I'd better come in."

They all went back into the drawing room. Ted and Kay had stopped dancing.

The door opened and a tall gaunt woman dressed in black came in. She said respectfully:

"Her ladyship's compliments and she would be glad to see Mr. Treves up in her room."

## VI

LADY TRESSILIAN received Mr. Treves with evident pleasure.

He and she were soon deep in an agreeable flood of reminiscences and a recalling of mutual acquaintances.

At the end of half an hour Lady Tressilian gave a deep sigh of satisfaction.

"Ah," she said, "I've enjoyed myself! There's nothing like exchanging gossip and remembering old scandals."

"A little malice," agreed Mr. Treves, "adds a certain savor to life."

"By the way," said Lady Tressilian, "what do you think of our example of the eternal triangle?"

Mr. Treves looked discreetly blank.

"Er—what triangle?"

"Don't tell me you haven't noticed it! Nevile and his wives."

"Oh, that! The present Mrs. Strange is a singularly attractive young woman."

"So is Audrey," said Lady Tressilian.

Mr. Treves admitted:

"She has charm—yes."

Lady Tressilian exclaimed:

"Do you mean to tell me you can understand a man leaving Audrey, who is a—a person of rare quality— for—for a *Kay?*"

Mr. Treves replied calmly:

"Perfectly. It happens frequently."

"Disgusting. I should soon grow tired of Kay if I

were a man and wish I had never made such a fool of myself!"

"That also happens frequently. These sudden passionate infatuations," said Mr. Treves, looking very passionless and precise himself, "are seldom of long duration."

"And then what happens?" demanded Lady Tressilian.

"Usually," said Mr. Treves, "the—er—parties adjust themselves. Quite often there is a second divorce. The man then marries a third party—someone of a sympathetic nature."

"Nonsense! Nevile isn't a Mormon—whatever some of your clients may be!"

"The remarriage of the original parties occasionally takes place."

Lady Tressilian shook her head.

"That, *no!* Audrey has too much pride."

"You think so?"

"I am sure of it. Do not shake your head in that aggravating fashion!"

"It has been my experience," said Mr. Treves, "that women possess little or no pride where love affairs are concerned. Pride is a quality often on their lips, but not apparent in their actions."

"You don't understand Audrey. She was violently in love with Nevile. Too much so, perhaps. After he left her for this girl (though I don't blame him entirely— the girl pursued him everywhere and you know what men are!) she never wanted to see him again."

Mr. Treves coughed gently.

"And yet," he said, "she is here!"

"Oh, well," said Lady Tressilian, annoyed. "I don't profess to understand these modern ideas. I imagine that Audrey is here just to show that she doesn't care, and that it doesn't matter!"

"Very likely," Mr. Treves stroked his jaw. "She can put it to herself that way, certainly."

"You mean," said Lady Tressilian, "that you think she is still hankering after Nevile and that—oh, *no!* I won't believe such a thing!"

"It could be," said Mr. Treves.

"I won't have it," said Lady Tressilian. "I won't have it in my house."

"You are already disturbed, are you not?" asked Mr. Treves shrewdly. "There is tension. I have felt it in the atmosphere."

"So you feel it too?" said Lady Tressilian sharply.

"Yes, I am puzzled, I must confess. The true feelings of the parties remain obscure, but in my opinion, there is gunpowder about. The explosion may come any minute."

"Stop talking like Guy Fawkes and tell me what to do," said Lady Tressilian.

Mr. Treves held up his hands.

"Really, I am at a loss to know what to suggest. There is, I feel sure, a focal point. If we could isolate that—but there is so much that remains obscure."

"I have no intention of asking Audrey to leave," said Lady Tressilian. "As far as my observation goes, she has behaved perfectly in a very difficult situation. She has been courteous but aloof. I consider her conduct irreproachable."

"Oh, quite," said Mr. Treves. "Quite. But it's having a most marked effect on young Nevile Strange all the same."

"Nevile," said Lady Tressilian, "is *not* behaving well. I shall speak to him about it. But I couldn't turn him out of the house for a moment. Matthew regarded him as practically his adopted son."

"I know."

Lady Tressilian sighed. She said in a lowered voice:

"You know that Matthew was drowned here?"

"Yes."

"So many people have been surprised at my remaining here. Stupid of them. I have always felt Matthew near to me here. The whole house is full of him. I should feel lonely and strange anywhere else." She paused and went on. "I hoped at first that it might not be very long before I joined him. Especially when my health began to fail. But it seems I am one of these creaking gates—these perpetual invalids who never die." She thumped her pillow angrily.

"It doesn't please me, I can tell you! I always hoped that when my time came, it would come quickly—that I should meet Death face to face—not feel him creeping along beside me, always at my shoulder—gradually forcing me to sink to one indignity after another of illness. Increased helplessness—increasing dependence on other people!"

"But very devoted people, I am sure. You have a faithful maid?"

"Barrett? The one who brought you up? The comfort of my life! A grim old battleax, absolutely devoted. She's been with me for years."

"And you are lucky, I should say, in having Miss Aldin."

"You are right. I am lucky in having Mary."

"She is a relation?"

"A distant cousin. One of those selfless creatures whose lives are continually being sacrificed to those of other people. She looked after her father—a clever man —but terribly exacting. When he died I begged her to make her home with me and I have blessed the day she came to me. You've no idea what horrors most companions are. Futile boring creatures. Driving one mad with their inanity. They are companions because they are fit for nothing better. To have Mary, who is a well-read intelligent woman, is marvelous. She has really a first-class brain—a man's brain— She has read widely and deeply and there is nothing she cannot discuss. And she is as clever domestically as she is intellectually. She runs the house perfectly and keeps the servants happy—she eliminates all quarrels and jealousies—I don't know how she does it—just tact, I suppose."

"She has been with you long?"

"Twelve years—no, more than that. Thirteen—fourteen—something like that. She has been a great comfort."

Mr. Treves nodded.

Lady Tressilian, watching him through half-closed lids, said suddenly:

"What's the matter? You're worried about something?"

"A trifle," said Mr. Treves. "A mere trifle. Your eyes are sharp."

"I like studying people," said Lady Tressilian. "I always knew at once if there was anything on Matthew's mind." She sighed and leaned back on her pillows. "I must say good night to you now—" It was a Queen's dismissal—nothing discourteous about it. "I am very tired. But it has been a great, great pleasure. Come and see me again soon."

"You may depend upon my taking advantage of those kind words. I only hope I have not talked too long."

"Oh, no. I always tire very suddenly. Ring my bell for me, will you, before you go."

Mr. Treves pulled gingerly at a large old-fashioned bell pull that ended in a huge tassel.

"Quite a survival," he remarked.

"My bell? Yes. No new-fangled electric bells for me. Half of the time they're out of order and you go on pressing away! This thing never fails. It rings in Barrett's room upstairs—the bell hangs over her bed. So there's never any delay in answering it. If there is I pull it again pretty quickly."

As Mr. Treves went out of the room he heard the bell pulled a second time and heard the tinkle of it somewhere above his head. He looked up and noticed the wires that ran along the ceiling. Barrett came hurriedly down a flight of stairs and passed him going to her mistress.

Mr. Treves went slowly downstairs not troubling with the little lift on the downward journey. His face was drawn into a frown of uncertainty.

He found the whole party assembled in the drawing room and Mary Aldin at once suggested bridge, but Mr. Treves refused politely on the plea that he must very shortly be starting home.

"My hotel," he said, "is old-fashioned. They do not expect anyone to be out after midnight."

"It's a long time from that—only half past ten," said Nevile. "They don't lock you out, I hope?"

"Oh, no. In fact I doubt if the door is locked at all at night. It is shut at nine o'clock but one has only to turn the handle and walk in. People seem very haphazard down here, but I suppose they are justified in trusting to the honesty of the local people."

"Certainly no one locks their door in the day time here," said Mary. "Ours stands wide open all day long —but we do lock it up at night."

"What's the Balmoral Court like?" asked Ted Latimer. "It looks a queer High Victorian atrocity of a building."

"It lives up to its name," said Mr. Treves. "And has good solid Victorian comfort. Good beds, good cooking—roomy Victorian wardrobes. Immense baths with mahogany surrounds."

"Weren't you saying that you were annoyed about something at first?" asked Mary.

"Ah, yes. I had carefully reserved by letter two rooms on the ground floor. I have a weak heart, you know, and stairs are forbidden me. When I arrived I was vexed to find the rooms were not available. Instead I was allotted two rooms (very pleasant rooms I must admit) on the top floor. I protested, but it seems that an old resident who had been going to Scotland this month, was ill and had been unable to vacate the rooms."

"Mrs. Lucan, I expect," said Mary.

"I believe that is the name. Under the circumstances, I had to make the best of things. Fortunately there is a good automatic lift—so that I have really suffered no inconvenience."

Kay said:

"Ted, why don't you come and stay at the Balmoral Court? You'd be much more accessible."

"Oh, I don't think it looks my kind of place."

"Quite right, Mr. Latimer," said Mr. Treves. "It would not be at all in your line of country."

For some reason or other Ted Latimer flushed.

"I don't know what you mean by that," he said.

Mary Aldin, sensing constraint, hurriedly made a remark about a case in the paper.

"I see they've detained a man in the Kentish Town trunk case—" she said.

"It's the second man they've detained," said Nevile. "I hope they've got the right one this time."

"They may not be able to hold him even if he is," said Mr. Treves.

"Insufficient evidence?" asked Royde.

"Yes."

"Still," said Kay, "I suppose they always get the evidence in the end."

"Not always, Mrs. Strange. You'd be surprised if you

knew how many of the people who have committed crimes are walking about the country free and unmolested."

"Because they've never been found out, you mean?"

"Not that only. There is a man"—he mentioned a celebrated case of two years back—"the police know who committed those child murders—know it without a shadow of doubt—but they are powerless. The man has been given an alibi by two people and though that alibi is false there is no proving it to be so. Therefore the murderer goes free."

"How dreadful," said Mary.

Thomas Royde knocked out his pipe and said in his quiet reflective voice, "That confirms what I have always thought—that there are times when one is justified in taking the law into one's own hands."

"What do you mean, Mr. Royde?"

Thomas began to refill his pipe. He looked thoughtfully down at his hands as he spoke in jerky disconnected sentences.

"Suppose you knew—of a dirty piece of work—knew that the man who did it isn't accountable to existing laws—that he's immune from punishment. Then I hold—that one is justified in executing sentence oneself."

Mr. Treves said warmly:

"A most pernicious doctrine, Mr. Royde! Such an action would be quite unjustifiable!"

"Don't see it. I'm assuming, you know, that the *facts* are proved—it's just that the *law* is powerless!"

"Private action is still not to be excused."

Thomas smiled—a very gentle smile.

"I don't agree," he said. "If a man ought to have his neck wrung I wouldn't mind taking the responsibility of wringing it for him!"

"And in turn would render yourself liable to the law's penalties!"

Still smiling, Thomas said: "I'd have to be careful, of course. . . . In fact one would have to go in for a certain amount of low cunning. . . ."

Audrey said in her clear voice:

"You'd be found out, Thomas."

"Matter of fact," said Thomas, "I don't think I should."

"I knew a case once," began Mr. Treves and stopped. He said apologetically: "Criminology is rather a hobby of mine, you know."

"Please go on," said Kay.

"I have had a fairly wide experience of criminal cases," said Mr. Treves. "Only a few of them have held any real interest. Most murderers have been lamentably uninteresting and very short-sighted. However! I could tell you of one interesting example."

"Oh, do," said Kay. "I like murders."

Mr. Treves spoke slowly, apparently choosing his words with great deliberation and care.

"The case concerned a child. I will not mention that child's age or sex. The facts were as follows: Two children were playing with bows and arrows. One child sent an arrow through the other child in a vital spot and death resulted. There was an inquest, the surviving child was completely distraught and the accident was commiserated and sympathy expressed for the unhappy author of the deed."

He paused.

"Was that all?" asked Ted Latimer.

"That was all. A regrettable accident. But there is, you see, another side to the story. A farmer, some time previously, happened to have passed up a certain path in a wood nearby. There, in a little clearing, he had noticed a child practicing with a bow and arrow."

He paused—to let his meaning sink in.

"You mean," said Mary Aldin incredulously, "that it was *not* an accident—that it was intentional?"

"I don't know," said Mr. Treves. "I have never known. But it was stated at the inquest that the children were unused to bows and arrows and in consequence shot wildly and ignorantly."

"And that was not so?"

"That, in the case of *one* of the children, was certainly not so!"

"What did the farmer do?" said Audrey breathlessly.

"He did nothing. Whether he acted rightly or not, I have never been sure. It was the future of a child that was at stake. A child, he felt, ought to be given the benefit of a doubt."

Audrey said:

"But you yourself have no doubt about what really happened?"

Mr. Treves said gravely:

"Personally, I am of the opinion that it was a particularly ingenious murder—a murder committed by a child and planned down to every detail beforehand."

Ted Latimer asked:

"Was there a reason?"

"Oh, yes, there was a motive. Childish teasings, unkind words—enough to foment hatred. Children hate easily—"

Mary exclaimed:

"But the deliberation of it."

Mr. Treves nodded.

"Yes, the deliberation of it was bad. A child, keeping that murderous intention in its heart, quietly practicing day after day and then the final piece of acting—the awkward shooting—the catastrophe, the pretense of grief and despair. It was all incredible—so incredible that probably it would not have been believed in court."

"What happened to—to the child?" asked Kay curiously.

"Its name was changed, I believe," said Mr. Treves. "After the publicity of the inquest that was deemed advisable. That child is a grown up person today—somewhere in the world. The question is, has it still got a murderer's heart?"

He added thoughtfully:

"It is a long time ago, but I would recognize my little murderer anywhere."

"Surely not," objected Royde.

"Oh, yes. There was a certain physical peculiarity— Well, I will not dwell on the subject. It is not a very pleasant one. I must really be on my way home."

He rose.

Mary said, "You will have a drink first?"

The drinks were on a table at the other end of the room. Thomas Royde, who was near them, stepped forward and took the stopper out of the whisky decanter.

"A whisky and soda, Mr. Treves? Latimer, what about you?"

Nevile said to Audrey in a low voice:

"It's a lovely evening. Come out for a little."

She had been standing by the window looking out at the moonlit terrace. He stepped past her and stood outside, waiting. She turned back into the room, shaking her head quickly.

"No, I'm tired. I—I think I'll go to bed."

She crossed the room and went out. Kay gave a wide yawn.

"I'm sleepy too. What about you, Mary?"

"Yes, I think so. Good night, Mr. Treves. Look after Mr. Treves, Thomas."

"Good night, Miss Aldin. Good night, Mrs. Strange."

"We'll be over for lunch tomorrow, Ted," said Kay. "We could bathe if it's still like this."

"Right. I'll be looking out for you. Good night, Miss Aldin."

The two women left the room.

Ted Latimer said agreeably to Mr. Treves, "I'm coming your way, sir. Down to the ferry, so I pass the hotel."

"Thank you, Mr. Latimer. I shall be glad of your escort."

Mr. Treves, although he had declared his intention of departing, seemed in no hurry. He sipped his drink with pleasant deliberation and devoted himself to the task of extracting information from Thomas Royde as to the conditions of life in Malaya.

Royde was monosyllabic in his answers. The everyday details of existence might have been secrets of national importance from the difficulty with which they were dragged from him. He seemed to be lost in some abstraction of his own, out of which he roused himself with difficulty to reply to his questioner.

Ted Latimer fidgeted. He looked bored, impatient, anxious to be gone.

Suddenly interrupting, he exclaimed, "I nearly forgot. I brought Kay over some gramophone records she wanted. They're in the hall. I'll get them. Will you tell her about them tomorrow, Royde?"

The other man nodded. Ted left the room.

"That young man has a restless nature," murmured Mr. Treves.

Royde grunted without replying.

"A friend, I think, of Mrs. Strange's?" pursued the old lawyer.

"Of Kay Strange's," said Thomas.

Mr. Treves smiled.

"Yes," he said. "I meant that. He would hardly be a friend of——the first Mrs. Strange."

Royde said emphatically:

"No, he wouldn't."

Then, catching the other's quizzical eye, he said, flushing a little, "What I mean is—"

"Oh, I quite understood what you meant, Mr. Royde. You yourself are a friend of Mrs. Audrey Strange, are you not?"

Thomas Royde slowly filled his pipe from his tobacco pouch. His eyes bent to his task, he said or rather mumbled:

"M—yes. More or less brought up together."

"She must have been a very charming young girl?"

Thomas Royde said something that sounded like "Um-yum."

"A little awkward having two Mrs. Stranges in the house?"

"Oh, yes—yes, rather."

"A difficult position for the original Mrs. Strange."

Thomas Royde's face flushed.

"Extremely difficult."

Mr. Treves leaned forward. His question popped out sharply.

*"Why did she come, Mr. Royde?"*

"Well—I suppose—" the other's voice was indistinct, "she—didn't like to refuse."

"To refuse whom?"

Royde shifted awkwardly.

"Well, as a matter of fact, I believe she always comes this time of year—beginning of September."

"And Lady Tressilian asked Nevile Strange and his new wife at the same time?" The old gentleman's voice held a nice note of political incredulity.

"As to that, I believe Nevile asked himself."

"He was anxious, then, for this—reunion?"

Royde shifted uneasily. He replied, avoiding the other's eye:

"I suppose so."

"Curious," said Mr. Treves.

"Stupid sort of thing to do," said Thomas Royde, goaded into longer speech.

"Somewhat embarrassing, one would have thought," said Mr. Treves.

"Oh, well—people do do that sort of thing nowadays," said Thomas Royde vaguely.

"I wonder," said Mr. Treves, "if it had been anybody else's idea?"

Royde stared.

"Whose else's could it have been?"

Mr. Treves sighed.

"There are so many kind friends about in the world—always anxious to arrange other people's lives for them—to suggest courses of action that are not in harmony—" He broke off as Nevile Strange strolled back through the French window. At the same moment Ted Latimer entered by the door from the hall.

"Hullo, Ted, what have you got there?" asked Nevile.

"Gramophone records for Kay. She asked me to bring them over."

"Oh, did she? She didn't tell me." There was just a moment of constraint between the two, then Nevile strolled over to the drink tray and helped himself to a whisky and soda. His face looked excited and unhappy and he was breathing deeply.

Someone in Mr. Treves' hearing had referred to Nevile as "that lucky beggar Strange—got everything in the world anyone could wish for." Yet he did not look, at this moment, at all a happy man.

Thomas Royde, with Nevile's re-entry, seemed to feel that his duties as host were over. He left the room without attempting to say good night and his walk was slightly more hurried than usual. It was almost an escape.

"A delightful evening," said Mr. Treves politely as he set down his glass. "Most—ah—instructive."

"Instructive?" Nevile raised his eyebrows slightly.

"Information re the Malay States," suggested Ted, smiling broadly. "Hard work dragging answers out of Taciturn Thomas."

"Extraordinary fellow, Royde," said Nevile. "I believe he's always been the same. Just smokes that awful old pipe of his and listens and says Um and Ah occasionally and looks wise like an owl."

"Perhaps he thinks the more," Mr. Treves. "And now I really must take my leave."

"Come and see Lady Tressilian again soon," said Nevile as he accompanied the two men to the hall. "You cheer her up enormously. She has so few contacts now with the outside world. She's wonderful, isn't she?"

"Yes, indeed. A most stimulating conversationalist."

Mr. Treves dressed himself carefully with overcoat and muffler and after renewed good nights, he and Ted Latimer set out together.

The Balmoral Court was actually only about a hundred yards away, around one curve of the road. It loomed up prim and forbidding, the first outpost of the straggling country street.

The ferry, for which Ted Latimer was bound, was two or three hundred yards further down, at a point where the river was at its narrowest.

Mr. Treves stopped at the door of the Balmoral Court and held out his hand.

"Good night, Mr. Latimer. You are staying down here much longer?"

Ted smiled with a flash of white teeth.

"That depends, Mr. Treves. I haven't had time to be bored—yet."

"No—no, so I should imagine. I suppose like most young people nowadays, boredom is what you dread most in the world, and yet, I can assure you, there are worse things."

"Such as?"

Ted Latimer's voice was soft and pleasant, but it held an undercurrent of something else—something not quite so easy to define.

"Oh, I leave it to your imagination, Mr. Latimer. I would not presume to give you advice, you know. The advice of such elderly fogeys as myself is invariably treated with scorn. Rightly, perhaps, who knows? But we old buffers like to think that experience has taught us something. We have noticed a good deal, you know, in the course of a lifetime."

A cloud had come over the face of the moon. The street was very dark. Out of the darkness, a man's figure came towards them walking up the hill.

It was Thomas Royde.

"Just been down to the ferry for a bit of a walk," he said indistinctly because of the pipe clenched between his teeth.

"This your pub?" he asked Mr. Treves. "Looks as though you were locked out."

"Oh, I don't think so," said Mr. Treves.

He turned the big brass door knob and the door swung back.

"We'll see you safely in," said Royde.

The three of them entered the hall. It was dimly lit with only one electric light. There was no one to be seen, and an odor of bygone dinner, rather dusty velvet, and good furniture polish met their nostrils.

Suddenly Mr. Treves gave an exclamation of annoyance.

On the lift in front of them hung a notice:

### LIFT OUT OF ORDER

"Dear me," said Mr. Treves. "How extremely vexing. I shall have to walk up those stairs."

"Too bad," said Royde. "Isn't there a service lift—luggage—all that?"

"I'm afraid not. This one is used for all purposes. Well, I must take it slowly, that is all. Good night to you both."

He started slowly up the wide staircase. Royde and Latimer wished him good night, then let themselves out into the dark street.

There was a moment's pause, then Royde said abruptly:

"Well, good night."

"Good night. See you tomorrow."

"Yes."

Ted Latimer strode lightly down the hill towards the ferry. Thomas Royde stood looking after him for a moment, then he walked slowly in the opposite direction towards Gull's Point.

The moon came out from behind the cloud and Saltcreek was once more bathed in silvery radiance.

## VII

"JUST LIKE SUMMER," murmured Mary Aldin.

She and Audrey were sitting on the beach just below the imposing edifice of the Easterhead Bay Hotel. Audrey wore a white swim suit and looked like a delicate ivory figurine. Mary had not bathed. A little way along from them Kay lay on her face, exposing her bronzed limbs and back to the sun.

"Ugh," she sat up. "The water's horribly cold," she said accusingly.

"Oh, well, it *is* September," said Mary.

"It's always cold in England," said Kay discontentedly. "How I wish we were in the south of France. That really is hot."

Ted Latimer from beyond her murmured:

"This sun here isn't a real sun."

"Aren't you going in at all, Mr. Latimer?" asked Mary.

Kay laughed.

"Ted never goes in the water. Just suns himself like a lizard."

She stretched out a toe and prodded him. He sprang up.

"Come and walk, Kay. I'm cold."

They went off together along the beach.

"Like a lizard? Rather an unfortunate comparison," murmured Mary Aldin, looking after them.

"Is that what you think of him?" asked Audrey.

Mary Aldin frowned.

"Not quite. A lizard suggests something quite tame. I don't think he is tame."

"No," said Audrey thoughtfully. "I don't think so either."

"How well they look together," said Mary, watching the retreating pair. "They match somehow, don't they?"

"I suppose they do."

"They like the same things," went on Mary. "And have the same opinions and—and use the same language. What a thousand pities it is that—"

She stopped.

Audrey said sharply:

"That what?"

Mary said slowly:

"I suppose I was going to say what a pity it was that Nevile and she ever met."

Audrey sat up stiffly. What Mary called to herself "Audrey's frozen look" had come over her face. Mary said quickly:

"I'm sorry, Audrey. I shouldn't have said that."

"I'd so much rather—not talk about it if you don't mind."

"Of course, of course. It was very stupid of me. I—I hoped you'd got over it, I suppose."

Audrey turned her head slowly. With a calm expressionless face she said:

"I assure you there is nothing to get over. I—I have no feeling of any kind in the matter. I hope—I hope with all my heart, that Kay and Nevile will always be very happy together."

"Well, that's very nice of you, Audrey."

"It isn't nice. It is—just true. But I do think it is—well—unprofitable to keep on going back over the past. 'It's a pity this happened—or that!' It's all over now. Why rake it up? We've got to go on living our lives in the present."

"I suppose," said Mary simply, "that people like Kay and Ted are exciting to me because—well, they are so different from anything or anyone that I have ever come across."

"Yes, I suppose they are."

"Even you," said Mary with sudden bitterness, "have lived and had experiences that I shall probably never have. I know you've been unhappy—very unhappy—but I can't help feeling that even that is better than—well—nothing. Emptiness!"

She said the last word with a fierce emphasis.

Audrey's wide eyes looked a little startled.

"I never dreamed you ever felt like that."

"Didn't you?" Mary Aldin laughed apologetically. "Oh, just a momentary fit of discontent, my dear. I didn't really mean it."

"It can't be very gay for you," said Audrey slowly. "Just living here with Camilla—dear thing though she is. Reading to her, managing the servants, never going away."

"I'm well fed and housed," said Mary. "Thousands of women aren't even that. And really, Audrey, I am quite contented. I have"—a smile played for a moment round her lips—"my private distractions."

"Secret vices?" asked Audrey, smiling also.

"Oh, I plan things," said Mary vaguely. "In my mind, you know. And I like experimenting sometimes—upon people. Just seeing, you know, if I can make them react to what I say in the way I mean."

"You sound almost sadistic, Mary. How little I really know you!"

"Oh, it's all quite harmless. Just a childish little amusement."

Audrey asked curiously:

"Have you experimented on me?"

"No. You're the only person I have always found quite incalculable. I never know, you see, what you are thinking."

"Perhaps," said Audrey gravely, "that is just as well."

She shivered and Mary exclaimed:

"You're cold."

"Yes. I think I will go and dress. After all, it *is* September."

Mary Aldin remained alone staring at the reflection on the water. The tide was going out. She stretched herself out on the sand closing her eyes.

They had had a good lunch at the hotel. It was still quite full although it was past the height of the season. A queer mixed-looking lot of people. Oh, well, it had been a day out. Something to break the monotony of day following day. It had been a relief, too, to get away from that sense of tension, that strung-up atmosphere that there had been lately at Gull's Point. It hadn't been Audrey's fault, but Nevile—

Her thoughts broke up abruptly as Ted Latimer plumped himself down on the beach beside her.

"What have you done with Kay?" Mary asked.

Ted replied briefly:

"She's been claimed by her legal owner."

Something in his tone made Mary Aldin sit up. She glanced across the stretch of shining golden sands to where Nevile and Kay were walking by the water's edge. Then she glanced quickly at the man beside her.

She had thought of him as meretricious, as queer, as dangerous, even. Now for the first time she got a glimpse of someone young and hurt. She thought:

"He was in love with Kay—really in love with her—and then Nevile came and took her away. . . ."

She said gently:

"I hope you are enjoying yourself down here."

They were conventional words. Mary Aldin seldom used any words but conventional ones—that was her language. But her tone was an offer—for the first time —of friendliness. Ted Latimer responded to it.

"As much, probably, as I should enjoy myself anywhere!"

Mary said:

"I'm sorry."

"But you don't care a damn, really! I'm an outsider —and what does it matter what outsiders feel and think?"

She turned her head to look at this bitter and handsome young man.

He returned her look with one of defiance.

She said slowly, as one who makes a discovery, "I see. You don't like us."

He laughed shortly. "Did you expect me to?"

She said thoughtfully:

"I suppose, you know, that I did expect just that— One takes, of course, too much for granted. One should be more humble. Yes, it would not have occurred to me that you would not like us. We have tried to make you welcome——as Kay's friend."

"Yes——as Kay's friend!"

The interruption came with a quick venom.

Mary said with disarming sincerity:

"I wish you would tell me——really I wish it——just why you dislike us? What have we done? What is wrong with us?"

Ted Latimer said, with a blistering emphasis on the one word:

"Smug!"

"Smug?" Mary queried it without rancor, examining the charge with judicial appraisement.

"Yes," she admitted. "I see that we could seem like that."

"You are like that. You take all the good things of life for granted. You're happy and superior in your little roped-off enclosure shut off from the common herd. You look at people like me as though I were one of the animals outside!"

"I'm sorry," said Mary.

"It's true, isn't it?"

"No, not quite. We are stupid, perhaps, and un-imaginative——but not malicious. I myself am conventional and superficially, I daresay, what you call smug. But really, you know, I'm quite human inside. I'm very sorry, this minute, because you are unhappy and I wish I could do something about it."

"Well——if that's so——it's nice of you."

There was a pause, then Mary said gently:

"Have you always been in love with Kay?"

"Pretty well."

"And she?"

"I thought so——until Strange came along."

Mary said gently:

"And you're still in love with her?"

"I should think that was obvious."

After a moment or two, Mary said quietly:

"Hadn't you better go away from here?"

"Why should I?"

"Because you are only letting yourself in for more unhappiness."

He looked at her and laughed.

"You're a nice creature," he said. "But you don't know much about the animals prowling about outside your little enclosure. Quite a lot of things may happen in the near future."

"What sort of things?" said Mary sharply.

He laughed.

"Wait and see."

## VIII

WHEN AUDREY had dressed she went along the beach and out along a jutting point of rocks, joining Thomas Royde who was sitting there smoking a pipe, exactly opposite to Gull's Point which stood white and serene on the opposite side of the river.

Thomas turned his head at Audrey's approach, but he did not move. She sat down beside him without speaking. They were silent with the comfortable silence of two people who know each other very well indeed.

"How near it looks," said Audrey at last, breaking the silence.

Thomas looked across at Gull's Point.

"Yes, we could swim home."

"Not at this tide. There was a housemaid Camilla had once. She was an enthusiastic bather, used to swim across and back whenever the tide was right. It has to be low or high—but when it's running out it sweeps you right down to the mouth of the river. It did that to her one day—only luckily she kept her head and came ashore all right on Easter Point—only very exhausted."

"It doesn't say anything about its being dangerous here."

"It isn't this side. The current is the other side. It's deep there under the cliffs. There was a would-be suicide last year—threw himself off Stark Head—but he got caught by a tree halfway down the cliff and the coast guards got to him all right."

"Poor devil," said Thomas. "I bet he didn't thank them. Must be sickening to have made up your mind to get out of it all and then be saved. Makes a fellow feel a fool."

"Perhaps he's glad now," suggested Audrey dreamily.

"I wonder."

Thomas puffed away at his pipe. By turning his head very slightly he could look at Audrey. He noted her grave absorbed face as she stared across the water. The long brown lashes that rested on the pure line of the cheek, the small shell-like ear—

That reminded him of something.

"Oh, by the way, I've got your earring—the one you lost last night."

His fingers delved into his pocket. Audrey stretched out a hand.

"Oh, good, where did you find it? On the terrace?"

"No. It was near the stairs. You must have lost it as you came down to dinner. I noticed you hadn't got it at dinner."

"I'm glad to have it back."

She took it. Thomas reflected that it was rather a large barbaric earring for so small an ear. The ones she had on today were large, too.

He remarked:

"You wear your earrings even when you bathe. Aren't you afraid of losing them?"

"Oh, these are very cheap things. I hate being without earrings because of this."

She touched her left ear. Thomas remembered.

"Oh, yes, that time old Bouncer bit you?"

Audrey nodded.

They were silent, reliving a childish memory. Audrey Standish (as she then was), a long spindle-legged child, putting her face down on old Bouncer who had had a sore paw. A nasty bite, he had given her. She had had to have a stitch put in it. Not that there was much to show now—just the tiniest little scar.

"My dear girl," he said. "You can hardly see the mark. Why do you mind?"

Audrey paused before answering with evident sincerity, "It's because—because I just can't bear a *blemish*."

Thomas nodded. It fitted in with his knowledge of Audrey—of her instinct for perfection. She was in herself so perfectly finished an article.

He said suddenly:

"You're far more beautiful than Kay."

She turned quickly.

"Oh, no, Thomas. Kay—Kay is really lovely."

"On the outside. Not underneath."

"Are you referring," said Audrey with faint amusement, "to my beautiful soul?"

Thomas knocked out the ashes of his pipe.

"No," he said. "I think I mean your bones."

Audrey laughed.

Thomas packed a new pipeful of tobacco. They were silent for quite five minutes, but Thomas glanced at Audrey more than once though he did it so unobtrusively that she was unaware of it.

He said at last quietly, "What's wrong, Audrey?"

"Wrong? What do you mean by wrong?"

"Wrong with you. There's something."

"No, there's nothing. Nothing at all."

"But there is."

She shook her head.

"Won't you tell me?"

"There's nothing to tell."

"I suppose I'm being a chump—but I've got to say it—" He paused. "Audrey—can't you forget about it? Can't you let it all go?"

She dug her small hands convulsively into the rock.

"You don't understand—you can't begin to understand."

"But, Audrey, my dear, I do. That's just it. I *know*."

She turned a small doubtful face to him.

"I know just exactly what you've been through. And —and what it must have meant to you."

She was very white now, white to the lips.

"I see," she said. "I didn't think—anyone knew."

"Well, I do. I—I'm not going to talk about it. But what I want to impress upon you is that it's all over— it's past and done with."

She said in a low voice:

"Some things don't pass."

"Look here, Audrey, it's no good brooding and remembering. Granted you've been through hell. It does no good to go over and over a thing in your mind. Look forward—not back. You're quite young. You've got your life to live and most of that life is in front of you. Think of tomorrow, not of yesterday."

She looked at him with a steady, wide-eyed gaze that was singularly unrevealing of her real thoughts.

"And supposing," she said, "that I can't do that."

"But you must."

Audrey said gently:

"I thought you didn't understand. I'm—I'm not quite normal about—some things, I suppose."

He broke in roughly, "Rubbish. You—" He stopped.

"I—what?"

"I was thinking of you as you were when you were a girl—before you married Nevile. Why did you marry Nevile?"

Audrey smiled.

"Because I fell in love with him."

"Yes, yes, I know that. But why did you fall in love with him? What attracted you to him so much?"

She crinkled her eyes as though trying to see through the eyes of a girl now dead.

"I think," she said, "it was because he was so 'positive.' He was so much the opposite of what I was, myself. I always felt shadowy—not quite real. Nevile was very real. And so happy and sure of himself and so— everything that I was not." She added with a smile: "And very good looking."

Thomas Royde said bitterly:

"Yes, the ideal Englishman—good at sports, modest, good looking, always the little pukka sahib—getting everything he wanted all along the line."

Audrey sat very upright and stared at him.

"You hate him," she said slowly. "You hate him very much, don't you?"

He avoided her eyes, turning away to cup a match in his hands as he relit the pipe that had gone out.

"Wouldn't be surprising if I did, would it?" he said indistinctly. "He's got everything that I haven't. He can play games, and swim and dance, and talk. And I'm a tongue-tied oaf with a crippled arm. He's always been brilliant and successful and I've always been a dull dog. And he married the only girl I ever cared for."

She made a faint sound. He said savagely:

"You've always known that, haven't you? You knew

I cared about you ever since you were fifteen. You know that I still care—"

She stopped him.

"No. Not now."

"What do you mean—not now?"

Audrey got up. She said in a quiet reflective voice:

"Because—now—I am different."

"Different in what way?"

He got up too and stood facing her.

Audrey said in a quick, rather breathless voice:

"If you don't know, I can't tell you. . . . I'm not always sure myself. I only know—"

She broke off and turning abruptly away, she walked quickly back over the rocks towards the hotel.

Turning a corner of the cliff, she came across Nevile. He was lying full length peering into a rock pool. He looked up and grinned.

"Hullo, Audrey."

"Hullo, Nevile."

"I'm watching a crab. Awfully active little beggar. Look, here he is."

She knelt down and stared where he pointed.

"See him?"

"Yes."

"Have a cigarette?"

She accepted one and he lighted it for her. After a moment or two, during which she did not look at him, he said nervously:

"I say, Audrey?"

"Yes."

"It's all right, isn't it? I mean—between us."

"Yes. Yes, of course."

"I mean—we're friends and all that."

"Oh, yes—yes, of course."

"I—I do want us to be friends."

He looked at her anxiously. She gave him a nervous smile.

He said conversationally:

"It's been a jolly day, hasn't it? Weather good and all that?"

"Oh, yes—yes."

"Quite hot really for September."

"Very."

There was a pause.

"Audrey—"

She got up.

"Your wife wants you, she's waving to you."

"Who—oh, Kay."

"I said your wife."

He scrambled to his feet and stood looking at her.

He said in a very low voice:

"You're my wife, Audrey. . . ."

She turned away. Nevile ran down on to the beach and across the sand to join Kay.

## IX

ON THEIR ARRIVAL back at Gull's Point, Hurstall came out into the hall and spoke to Mary.

"Would you go up at once to her ladyship, Miss? She is feeling very upset and wanted to see you as soon as you got in."

Mary hurried up the stairs. She found Lady Tressilian looking white and shaken.

"Dear Mary, I am so glad you have come. I am feeling most distressed. Poor Mr. Treves is dead."

"Dead?"

"Yes, isn't it terrible? So sudden. Apparently he didn't even get undressed last night. He must have collapsed as soon as he got home."

"Oh, dear, I am sorry."

"One knows, of course, that he was delicate. A weak heart. I hope nothing happened while he was here to overstrain it? There was nothing indigestible for dinner?"

"I don't think so—no, I am sure there wasn't. He seemed quite well and in good spirits."

"I am really very distressed. I wish, Mary, that you would go to the Balmoral Court and make a few inquiries of Mrs. Rogers. Ask her if there is anything we can do? And then the funeral. For Matthew's sake I would like to do anything we could. These things are so awkward at a hotel."

Mary spoke firmly.

"Dear Camilla, you really must not worry. This has been a shock to you."

"Indeed it has."

"I will go to the Balmoral Court at once and then come back and tell you all about things."

"Thank you, Mary dear, you are always so practical and understanding."

"Please try and rest now. A shock of this kind is so bad for you."

Mary Aldin left the room and came downstairs. Entering the drawing room she exclaimed:

"Old Mr. Treves is dead. He died last night after returning home."

"Poor old boy," exclaimed Nevile. "What was it?"

"Heart apparently. He collapsed as soon as he got in."

Thomas Royde said thoughtfully:

"I wonder if the stairs did him in."

"Stairs?" Mary looked at him inquiringly.

"Yes. When Latimer and I left him, he was just starting up. We told him to take it slow."

Mary exclaimed:

"But how very foolish of him not to take the lift."

"The lift was out of order."

"Oh, I see. How very unfortunate. Poor old man."

She added: "I am going round there now. Camilla wants to know if there is anything we can do."

Thomas said: "I'll come with you."

They walked together down the road and round the corner to the Balmoral Court. Mary remarked:

"I wonder if he has any relatives who ought to be notified."

"He didn't mention anyone."

"No, and people usually do. They say 'my niece,' or 'my cousin.'"

"Was he married?"

"I believe not."

They entered the open door of the Balmoral Court. Mrs. Rogers, the proprietress, was talking to a tall middle-aged man, who raised a friendly hand in greeting to Mary.

"Good afternoon, Miss Aldin."

"Good afternoon, Dr. Lazenby. This is Mr. Royde. We came round with a message from Lady Tressilian to know if there is anything we can do."

"That's very kind of you, Miss Aldin," said the hotel proprietress. "Come into my room, won't you?"

They all went into the small comfortable sitting room and Dr. Lazenby said:

"Mr. Treves was dining at your place last night, wasn't he?"

"Yes."

"How did he seem? Did he show any signs of distress?"

"No, he seemed very well and cheerful."

The doctor nodded.

"Yes, that's the worst of these heart cases. The end is nearly always sudden. I had a look at his prescriptions upstairs and it seems quite clear that he was in a very precarious state of health. I shall communicate with his London doctor, of course."

"He was very careful of himself always," said Mrs. Rogers. "And I'm sure he had every care here we could give him."

"I'm sure of that, Mrs. Rogers," said the doctor tactfully. "It was just some tiny additional strain, no doubt."

"Such as walking upstairs," suggested Mary.

"Yes, that might do it. In fact almost certainly would —that is, if he ever walked up those three flights—but surely he never did do anything of that kind?"

"Oh, no," said Mrs. Rogers. "He always used the lift. Always. He was most particular."

"I mean," said Mary, "that with the lift being out of order last night—"

Mrs. Rogers was staring at her in surprise.

"But the lift wasn't out of order at all yesterday, Miss Aldin."

Thomas Royde coughed.

"Excuse me," he said. "I came home with Mr. Treves last night. There was a placard on the lift saying 'Out of Order.'"

Mrs. Rogers stared.

"Well, that's an odd thing. I'd have declared there was nothing wrong with the lift—in fact I'm sure there wasn't. I'd have heard about it if there was. We haven't had anything go wrong with the lift (touching wood) since—oh, not for a good eighteen months. Very reliable it is."

"Perhaps," suggested the doctor, "some porter or hall boy put that notice up when he was off duty?"

"It's an automatic lift, Doctor, it doesn't need anyone to work it."

"Ah, yes, so it is. I was forgetting."

"I'll have a word with Joe," said Mrs. Rogers. She bustled out of the room calling, "Joe—Joe."

Dr. Lazenby looked curiously at Thomas.

"Excuse me, you're quite sure, Mr.—er—"

"Royde," put in Mary.

"Quite sure," said Thomas.

Mrs. Rogers came back with the porter. Joe was emphatic that nothing whatever had been wrong with the lift on the preceding night. There was such a placard as Thomas had described—but it was tucked away under the desk and hadn't been used for over a year.

They all looked at each other and agreed it was a most mysterious thing. The doctor suggested some practical joke on the part of one of the hotel visitors, and perforce they left it at that.

In reply to Mary's inquiries, Dr. Lazenby explained that Mr. Treves' chauffeur had given him the address of Mr. Treves' solicitors, and he was communicating with them and that he would come round and see Lady Tressilian and tell her what was going to be done about the funeral.

Then the busy cheerful doctor hurried off and Mary and Thomas walked slowly back to Gull's Point.

Mary said:

"You're quite sure you saw that notice, Thomas?"

"Both Latimer and I saw it."

"What an extraordinary thing!" said Mary.


X


IT WAS THE twelfth of September.

"Only two more days," said Mary Aldin.

Then she bit her lip and flushed.

Thomas Royde looked at her thoughtfully.

"Is that how you feel about it?"

"I don't know what's the matter with me," said Mary. "Never in all my life have I been so anxious for a visit to come to an end. And usually we enjoy having Nevile so much. And Audrey too."

Thomas nodded.

"But this time," went on Mary, "one feels as though one were sitting on dynamite. At any minute the whole thing may explode. That's why I said to myself first thing this morning: 'Only two days more.' Audrey goes on Wednesday and Nevile and Kay on Thursday."

"And I go on Friday," said Thomas.

"Oh, I'm not counting you. You've been a tower of strength. I don't know what I should have done without you."

"The human buffer?"

"More than that. You've been so calm and so—so kind. That sounds rather ridiculous but it really does express what I mean."

Thomas looked pleased though slightly embarrassed.

"I don't know why we've all been so het up," said Mary reflectively. "After all, if there was an—an outburst—it would be awkward and embarrassing, but nothing more."

"But there's been more to your feeling than that."

"Oh, yes, there has. A definite feeling of apprehension. Even the servants feel it. The kitchenmaid burst into tears and gave notice this morning—for no reason at all. The cook's jumpy—Hurstall is all on edge—even Barrett who is usually as calm as a—a battleship—has shown signs of nerves. And all because Nevile had this ridiculous idea of wanting his former and his present wife to make friends and so soothe his own conscience."

"In which ingenious idea he has singularly failed," remarked Thomas.

"Yes. Kay is—is getting quite beside herself. And really, Thomas, I can't help sympathizing with her."

She paused. "Did you notice the way Nevile looked after Audrey as she went up the stairs last night? He still cares about her, Thomas. The whole thing has been the most tragic mistake."

Thomas started filling his pipe.

"He should have thought of that before," he said in a hard voice.

"Oh, I know. That's what one says. But it doesn't alter the fact that the whole thing is a tragedy. I can't help feeling sorry for Nevile."

"People like Nevile—" began Thomas and then stopped.

"Yes?"

"People like Nevile think that they can always have everything their own way—and have everything they want, too. I don't suppose Nevile has ever had a setback over anything in his life till he came up against this business of Audrey. Well, he's got it now. He can't have Audrey. She's out of his reach. No good his making a song and dance about it. He's just got to lump it."

"I suppose you're quite right. But you do sound hard. Audrey was so much in love with Nevile when she married him—and they always got on together so well."

"Well, she's out of love with him now."

"I wonder," murmured Mary under her breath.

Thomas was going on:

"And I'll tell you something else. Nevile had better look out for Kay. She's a dangerous kind of young woman—really dangerous. If she got her temper up she'd stop at nothing."

"Oh, dear," Mary sighed and, returning to her original remark, said hopefully: "Well, it's only two days more."

Things had been very difficult for the last four or five days. The death of Mr. Treves had given Lady Tressilian a shock which had told adversely on her health. The funeral had taken place in London for which Mary was thankful, since it enabled the old lady to take her mind off the sad event more quickly than she might have been able to do otherwise. The domestic side of the household had been nervy and difficult and Mary really felt tired and dispirited this morning.

"It's partly the weather," she said aloud. "It's unnatural."

It had indeed been an unusually hot and fine spell for September. On several days the thermometer had registered 70 in the shade.

Nevile strolled out of the house and joined them as she spoke.

"Blaming the weather?" he asked with a glance up at the sky. "It is rather incredible. Hotter than ever today. And no wind. Makes one feel jumpy somehow. However I think we'll get rain before very long. Today is just a bit too tropical to last."

Thomas Royde had moved very gently and aimlessly away and now disappeared round the corner of the house.

"Departure of gloomy Thomas," said Nevile. "Nobody could say he shows any enjoyment of my company."

"He's rather a dear," said Mary.

"I disagree. Narrow-minded prejudiced sort of chap."

"He always hoped to marry Audrey, I think. And then you came along and cut him out."

"It would have taken him about seven years to make up his mind to ask her to marry him. Did he expect the poor girl to wait about while he made up his mind?"

"Perhaps," said Mary deliberately, "it will all come right now."

Nevile looked at her and raised an eyebrow.

"True love rewarded? Audrey marry that wet fish?

She's a lot too good for that. No, I don't see Audrey
marrying gloomy Thomas."

"I believe she is really very fond of him, Nevile."

"What matchmakers you women always are! Can't
you let Audrey enjoy her freedom for a bit?"

"If she does enjoy it, certainly."

Nevile said quickly:

"You think she's not happy?"

"I really haven't the least idea."

"No more have I," said Nevile slowly. "One never
does know what Audrey is feeling." He paused and
then added, "But Audrey is one hundred per cent thor-
oughbred. She's white all through."

Then he said, more to himself than to Mary, "God,
what a damned fool I've been!"

Mary went into the house a little worried. For the
third time she repeated to herself the comforting words,
"Only two days more."

Nevile wandered restlessly about the garden and
terraces.

Right at the end of the garden he found Audrey sitting on the low wall looking down at the water below.
It was high tide and the river was full.

She got up at once and came towards him.

"I was just coming back to the house. It must be
nearly teatime."

She spoke quickly and nervously without looking at
him.

He walked beside her without speaking.

Only when they reached the terrace again did he
say:

"Can I talk to you, Audrey?"

She said at once, her fingers gripping the edge of the
balustrade:

"I think you'd better not."

"That means you know what I want to say."

She did not answer.

"What about it, Audrey? Can't we go back to where we were? Forget everything that has happened?"

"Including Kay?"

"Kay," said Nevile, "will be sensible."

"What do you mean by sensible?"

"Simply this. I shall go to her and tell her the truth. Fling myself on her generosity. Tell her, what is true, that you are the only woman I ever loved."

"You loved Kay when you married her."

"My marriage to Kay was the biggest mistake I ever made. I—"

He stopped. Kay had come out of the drawing room window. She walked towards them, and before the fury in her eyes even Nevile shrank a little!

"Sorry to interrupt this touching scene," said Kay. "But I think it's about time I did."

Audrey got up and moved away.

"I'll leave you alone," she said.

Her face and voice were colorless.

"That's right," said Kay. "You've done all the mischief you wanted to do, haven't you? I'll deal with you later. Just now I'd rather have it out with Nevile."

"Look here, Kay, Audrey has absolutely nothing to do with this. It's not her fault. Blame me if you like—"

"And I do like," said Kay. Her eyes blazed at Nevile. "What sort of a man do you think you are?"

"A pretty poor sort of man," said Nevile bitterly.

"You leave your wife, come bullheaded after me, get your wife to give you a divorce. Crazy about me one minute, tired of me the next! Now I suppose you want to go back to that whey-faced, mewling, double-crossing little cat—"

"Stop that, Kay!"

"Well, what do you want?"

Nevile was very white. He said:

"I'm every kind of a worm you like to call me. But it's no good, Kay. *I can't go on.* I think—really—I must have loved Audrey all the time. My love for you was—was a kind of madness. But it's no good, my dear—you and I don't belong. I shouldn't be able to make you happy in the long run. Believe me, Kay, it's better to cut our losses. Let's try and part friends. Be generous."

Kay said in a deceptively quiet voice:

"What exactly are you suggesting?"

Nevile did not look at her. His chin took on a dogged angle.

"We can get a divorce. You can divorce me for desertion."

"Not for some time. You'll have to wait for it."

"I'll wait," said Nevile.

"And then, after three years or whatever it is, you'll ask dear sweet Audrey to marry all over again?"

"If she'll have me."

"She'll have you all right!" said Kay viciously. "And where do I come in?"

"You'll be free to find a better man than I am. Naturally I shall see you're well provided for—"

"Cut out the bribes!" Her voice rose, as she lost control of herself:

"Listen to me, Nevile. You can't do this thing to me! I'll not divorce you. I married you because I loved you. I know when you started turning against me. It was after I let you know I followed you to Estoril. You wanted to think it was all Fate. It upset your vanity to think it was *me!* Well, I'm not ashamed of what I did. You fell in love with me and married me and I'm not going to let you go back to that sly little cat who's got her hooks into you again. She meant this to happen—but she's not going to bring it off! I'll kill you first. Do you hear? I'll kill you. I'll kill her too. I'll see you both dead. I'll—"

Nevile took a step forward and caught her by the arm.

"Shut up, Kay. For goodness' sake. You can't make this kind of scene here."

"Can't I? You'll see. I'll—"

Hurstall stepped out on the terrace. His face was quite impassive.

"Tea is served in the drawing room," he announced.

Kay and Nevile walked slowly towards the drawing room window.

Hurstall stood aside to let them pass in.

Up in the sky the clouds were gathering.


## XI

THE RAIN started falling at a quarter to seven. Nevile watched it from the window of his bedroom. He had had no further conversation with Kay. They had avoided each other after tea.

Dinner that evening was a stilted difficult meal. Nevile was sunk in abstraction; Kay's face had an unusual amount of make-up; Audrey sat like a frozen ghost. Mary Aldin did her best to keep some kind of conversation going and was slightly annoyed with Thomas Royde for not playing up to her better.

Hurstall was nervous and his hands trembled as he handed the vegetables.

As the meal drew to a close, Nevile said with elaborate casualness, "Think I shall go over to Easterhead after dinner and look up Latimer. We might have a game of billiards."

"Take the latch key," said Mary. "In case you're back late."

"Thanks, I will."

They went into the drawing room where coffee was served.

The turning on of the wireless and the news was a welcome diversion.

Kay, who had been yawning ostentatiously ever since dinner, said she would go up to bed. She had got a headache.

"Have you got any aspirin?" asked Mary.

"Yes, thank you."

She left the room.

Nevile tuned the wireless on to a program with music. He sat silent on the sofa for some time. He did not look once at Audrey, but sat huddled up looking like an unhappy little boy. Against her will, Mary felt quite sorry for him.

"Well," he said at last, rousing himself. "Better be off if I'm going."

"Are you taking your car or going by ferry?"

"Oh, ferry. No sense in going a round of fifteen miles. I shall enjoy a bit of a walk."

"It's raining, you know."

"I know. I've got a Burberry."

He went towards the door.

"Good night."

In the hall, Hurstall came to him.

"If you please, sir, will you go up to Lady Tressilian? She wants to see you specially."

Nevile glanced at the clock. It was already ten o'clock.

He shrugged his shoulders and went upstairs and along the corridor to Lady Tressilian's room and tapped on the door. While he waited for her to say come in, he heard the voices of the others in the hall down below. Everybody was going to bed early tonight, it seemed.

"Come in," said Lady Tressilian's clear voice.

Nevile went in, shutting the door behind him.

Lady Tressilian was all ready for the night. All the lights were extinguished except one reading lamp by her bed. She had been reading, but she now laid down the book. She looked at Nevile over the top of her spectacles. It was, somehow, a formidable glance.

"I want to speak to you, Nevile," she said.

In spite of himself, Nevile smiled faintly.

"Yes, Headmaster," he said.

Lady Tressilian did not smile.

"There are certain things, Nevile, that I will not permit in my house. I have no wish to listen to anybody's private conversations but if you and your wife insist on shouting at each other exactly under my bedroom windows, I can hardly fail to hear what you say. I gather that you were outlining a plan whereby Kay was to divorce you and in due course you would remarry Audrey. That, Nevile, is a thing you simply cannot do and I will not hear of it for a moment."

Nevile seemed to be making an effort to control his temper.

"I apologize for the scene," he said, shortly. "As for the rest of what you say, surely that is my business!"

"No, it is not. You have used my house in order to get into touch with Audrey—or else Audrey has used it—"

"She has done nothing of the sort. She—"

Lady Tressilian stopped him with upraised hand.

"Anyway you can't do this thing, Nevile. Kay is your wife. She has certain rights of which you cannot deprive her. In this matter, I am entirely on Kay's side. You have made your bed and must lie upon it. Your duty now is to Kay and I am telling you so plainly—"

Nevile took a step forward. His voice rose:

"This is nothing whatever to do with you—"

"What is more," Lady Tressilian swept on regardless of his protest, "Audrey leaves this house tomorrow—"

"You can't do that! I won't stand for it—"

"Don't shout at me, Nevile."

"I tell you I won't have it—"

Somewhere along the passage a door shut. . . .

## XII

ALICE BENTHAM, the gooseberry-eyed housemaid, came to Mrs. Spicer the cook, in some perturbation.

"Oh, Mrs. Spicer, I don't rightly know what I ought to do."

"What's the matter, Alice?"

"It's Miss Barrett. I took her in her cup of tea over an hour ago. Fast asleep she was and never woke up, but I didn't like to do much. And then, five minutes ago, I went in again because she hadn't come down and her ladyship's tea all ready and waiting for her to take in. So I went in again and she's sleeping ever so—I can't stir her."

"Have you shaken her?"

"Yes, Mrs. Spicer. I shook her hard—but she just goes on lying there and she's ever such a horrid color."

"Goodness, she's not dead, is she?"

"Oh, no, Mrs. Spicer, because I can hear her breathing, but it's funny breathing. I think she's ill or something."

"Well, I'll go up and see myself. You take in her ladyship's tea. Better make a fresh pot. She'll be wondering what's happened."

Alice obediently did as she was told whilst Mrs. Spicer went up to the second floor.

Taking the tray along the corridor, Alice knocked at Lady Tressilian's door. After knocking twice and getting no answer she went in. A moment later, there was a crash of broken crockery and a series of wild screams and Alice came rushing out of the room and down the stairs to where Hurstall was crossing the hall to the dining room.

"Oh, Mr. Hurstall—there've been burglars and her ladyship's dead—killed—with a great hole in her head and blood everywhere...."

# A FINE
# ITALIAN HAND . . .

## *I*

SUPERINTENDENT BATTLE had enjoyed his holiday. There were still three days of it to run and he was a little disappointed when the weather changed and the rain fell. Still, what else could you expect in England? And he'd been extremely lucky up to now.

He was breakfasting with Inspector James Leach, his nephew, when the telephone rang.

"I'll come right along, sir." Jim put the receiver back.

"Serious?" asked Superintendent Battle. He noted the expression on his nephew's face.

"We've got a murder. Lady Tressilian. An old lady, very well known down here, an invalid. Has that house at Saltcreek that hangs right over the cliff."

Battle nodded.

"I'm going along to see the old man" (thus disrespectfully did Leach speak of his Chief Constable).

"He's a friend of hers. We're going to the place together."

As he went to the door he said pleadingly:

"You'll give me a hand, won't you, Uncle, over this? First case of this kind I've had."

"As long as I'm here, I will. Case of robbery and housebreaking, is it?"

"I don't know yet."


## II


HALF AN HOUR later, Major Robert Mitchell, the Chief Constable, was speaking gravely to uncle and nephew.

"It's early to say as yet," he said, "but one thing seems clear. This wasn't an outside job. Nothing taken, no signs of breaking in. All the windows and doors found shut this morning."

He looked directly at Battle.

"If I were to ask Scotland Yard, do you think they'd put you on the job? You're on the spot, you see. And then there's your relationship with Leach here. That is, if you're willing. It means cutting the end of your holiday."

"That's all right," said Battle. "As for the other, sir, you'll have to put it up to Sir Edgar" (Sir Edgar Cotton was Assistant Commissioner) "but I believe he's a friend of yours?"

Mitchell nodded.

"Yes, I think I can manage Edgar all right. That's settled, then! I'll get through right away."

He spoke into the telephone: "Get me the Yard."

"You think it's going to be an important case, sir?" asked Battle.

Mitchell said gravely:

"It's going to be a case where we don't want the possibility of making a mistake. We want to be absolutely sure of our man—or woman, of course."

Battle nodded. He understood quite well that there was something behind the words.

"Thinks he knows who did it," he said to himself. "And doesn't relish the prospect. Somebody well known and popular or I'll eat my boots!"

### III

BATTLE AND LEACH stood in the doorway of the well-furnished, handsome bedroom. On the floor in front of them a police officer was carefully testing for fingerprints the handle of a golf club—a heavy niblick. The head of the club was bloodstained and had one or two white hairs sticking to it.

By the bed Dr. Lazenby, who was police surgeon for the district, was bending over the body of Lady Tressilian.

He straightened up with a sigh.

"Perfectly straightforward. She was hit from in front with terrific force. First blow smashed in the bone and killed her, but the murderer struck again to make sure. I won't give you the fancy terms—just the plain horse sense of it."

"How long has she been dead?" asked Leach.

"I'd put it between ten o'clock and midnight."

"You can't go nearer than that?"

"I'd rather not. All sorts of factors to take into account. We don't hang people on *rigor mortis* nowadays. *Not earlier than ten, not later than midnight.*"

"And she was hit with this niblick?"

The doctor glanced over at it.

"Presumably. Luck, though, that the murderer left it

behind. I couldn't have deduced a niblick from the wound. As it happens the sharp edge of the club didn't touch the head—it was the angled back of the club that must have hit her."

"Wouldn't that have been rather difficult to do?" asked Leach.

"If it had been done on purpose, yes," agreed the doctor. "I can only suppose, that by a rather odd chance, it just happened that way."

Leach was raising his hands, instinctively trying to reconstruct the blow.

"Awkward," he commented.

"Yes," said the doctor thoughtfully. "The whole thing was awkward. She was struck, you see, on the right temple—but whoever did it must have stood on the right hand side of the bed—facing the head of the bed—there's no room on the left, the angle from the wall is too small."

Leach pricked up his ears.

"Left handed?" he queried.

"You won't get me to commit myself on that point," said Lazenby. "Far too many snags. I'll say, if you like, that the easiest explanation is that the murderer was left handed—but there are other ways of accounting for it. Suppose, for instance, the old lady had turned her head slightly to the left just as the man hit. Or he may have previously moved the bed out, stood on the left of it and afterwards moved the bed back."

"Not very likely—that last."

"Perhaps not, but it *might* have happened. I've had some experience in these things, and I can tell you, my boy, deducing that a murderous blow was struck left handed is full of pitfalls!"

Detective Sergeant Jones from the floor, remarked, "This golf club is the ordinary right-handed kind."

Leach nodded. "Still, it mayn't have belonged to the man who used it. It *was* a man, I suppose, Doctor?"

"Not necessarily. If the weapon was that heavy niblick a woman could have landed a terrible swipe with it."

Superintendent Battle said in his quiet voice:

"But you couldn't swear that that was the weapon, could you, Doctor?"

Lazenby gave him a quick interested glance.

"No. I can only swear that it *might* have been the weapon, and that presumably it *was* the weapon. I'll analyze the blood on it, make sure that it's the same blood group—also the hairs."

"Yes," said Battle approvingly. "It's always as well to be thorough."

Lazenby asked curiously:

"Got any doubts about that golf club yourself, Superintendent?"

Battle shook his head.

"Oh, no, no. I'm a simple man. Like to believe the thing I see with my eyes. She was hit with something heavy—that's heavy. It has blood and hair on it, therefore presumably her blood and hair. Ergo—that was the weapon used."

Leach asked:

"Was she awake or asleep when she was hit?"

"In my opinion, awake. There's astonishment on her face. I'd say—this is just a private personal opinion—that she didn't expect what was going to happen. There's no sign of any attempt to fight—and no horror or fear. I'd say off hand that either she had just woken up from sleep and was hazy and didn't take things in—or else she recognized her assailant as someone who could not possibly wish to harm her."

"The bedside lamp was on and nothing else," said Leach thoughtfully.

"Yes, that cuts either way. She may have turned it on when she was suddenly woken up by someone entering her room. Or it may have been on already."

Detective Sergeant Jones rose to his feet. He was smiling appreciatively.

"Lovely set of prints on that club," he said. "Clear as anything!"

Leach gave a deep sigh.

"That ought to simplify things."

"Obliging chap," said Dr. Lazenby. "Left the weapon —left his fingerprints on it—wonder he didn't leave his visiting card!"

"It might be," said Superintendent Battle, "that he just lost his head. Some do."

The doctor nodded.

"True enough. Well, I must go and look after my other patient."

"What patient?" Battle sounded suddenly interested.

"I was sent for by the butler before this was discovered. Lady Tressilian's maid was found in a coma this morning."

"What was wrong with her?"

"Heavily doped with one of the barbiturates. She's pretty bad, but she'll pull round."

"The maid?" said Battle. His rather ox-like eyes went heavily to the big bell pull, the tassel of which rested on the pillow near the dead woman's hand.

Lazenby nodded.

"Exactly. That's the first thing Lady Tressilian would have done if she'd cause to feel alarm—pull that bell and summon the maid. Well, she could have pulled it till all was blue. The maid wouldn't have heard."

"That was taken care of, was it?" said Battle. "You're sure of that? She wasn't in the habit of taking sleeping draughts?"

"I'm positive she wasn't. There's not a sign of such

a thing in her room. And I've found out how it was given to her. Senna pods. She drank off a brew of senna pods every night. The stuff was in that."

Superintendent Battle scratched his chin.

"H'm," he said. "Someone knew all about this house. You know, Doctor, this is a very odd sort of murder."

"Well," said Lazenby. "That's *your* business."

"He's a good man, our doctor," said Leach when Lazenby had left the room.

The two men were alone now. The photographs had been taken, and measurements recorded. The two police officers knew every fact that was to be known about the room where the crime had been committed.

Battle nodded in answer to his nephew's remark. He seemed to be puzzling over something.

"Do you think anyone could have handled that club—with gloves on, say—after those fingerprints were made?"

Leach shook his head.

"I don't and no more do you. You couldn't grasp that club—not *use* it, I mean, without smearing those prints. They weren't smeared. They were clear as clear. You saw for yourself."

Battle agreed.

"And now we ask very nicely and politely if everyone will allow us to take their fingerprints—no compulsion, of course. And everybody will say yes—and then one of two things will happen. Either none of these fingerprints will agree, or else—"

"Or else we'll have got our man?"

"I suppose so. Or our woman, perhaps."

Leach shook his head.

"No, not a woman. Those prints on the clubs were a man's. Too big for a woman's. Besides this isn't a woman's crime."

"No," agreed Battle. "Quite a man's crime. Brutal,

masculine, rather athletic and slightly stupid. Know anybody in the house like that?"

"I don't know anyone in the house yet. They're all together in the dining room."

Battle moved towards the door.

"We'll go and have a look at them." He glanced over his shoulder at the bed, shook his head and remarked:

"I don't like that bell pull."

"What about it?"

"It doesn't fit."

He added as he opened the door:

"Who wanted to kill her, I wonder? A lot of cantankerous old ladies about just asking for a tap on the skull. She doesn't look that sort. I should think she was *liked*." He paused a minute and then asked:

"Well off, wasn't she? Who gets her money?"

Leach answered the implication of the words:

"You've hit it! That will be the answer. It's one of the first things to find out."

As they went downstairs together, Battle glanced at the list in his hand.

He read out:

"Miss Aldin, Mr. Royde, Mr. Strange, Mrs. Strange, Mrs. Audrey Strange. H'm, seem a lot of the Strange family."

"Those are his two wives, I understand."

Battle's eyebrows rose and he murmured:

"Bluebeard, is he?"

The family were assembled round the dining room table, where they had made a pretense of eating.

Superintendent Battle glanced keenly at the faces turned to him. He was sizing them up after his own peculiar methods. His view of them might have surprised them had they known it. It was a sternly biased view. No matter what the law pretends as to regarding people innocent until they are proved guilty, Superintendent Battle always regarded everyone connected with a murder case as a potential murderer.

He glanced from Mary Aldin sitting upright and pale at the head of the table, to Thomas Royde filling a pipe beside her, to Audrey sitting with her chair pushed back, a coffee cup and saucer in her right hand, a cigarette in her left, to Nevile looking dazed and bewildered, trying with a shaking hand to light a cigarette, to Kay with her elbows on the table and the pallor of her face showing through her make-up.

These were Superintendent Battle's thoughts:

Suppose that's Miss Aldin. Cool customer—competent woman, I should say. Won't catch her off her guard easily. Man next to her is a dark horse—got a groggy arm—bit of a poker face—got an inferiority complex as likely as not. That's one of these wives, I suppose—she's scared to death—yes, she's scared all right. Funny about that coffee cup. That's Strange, I've seen him before somewhere. He's got the jitters all right—nerves shot to pieces. Redheaded girl's a tartar—devil of a temper. Brains as well as temper, though.

Whilst he was thus sizing them up, Inspector Leach was making a stiff little speech. Mary Aldin mentioned everyone present by name.

She ended up:

"It has been a terrible shock to us, of course, but we are anxious to help you in any way we can."

"To begin with," said Leach, holding it up, "does anybody know anything about this golf club?"

With a little cry, Kay said, "How horrible. Is that what—" and stopped.

Nevile Strange got up and came round the table.

"Looks like one of mine. Can I just see?"

"It's quite all right *now*," said Inspector Leach. "You can handle it."

That little significant "now" did not seem to produce

any reaction in the onlookers. Nevile examined the club.

"I think it's one of the niblicks out of my bag," he said. "I can tell you for sure in a minute or two. If you will just come with me." They followed him to a big cupboard under the stairs. He flung open the door of it and to Battle's confused eyes it seemed literally crowded with tennis rackets. At the same time, he remembered where he had seen Nevile Strange. He said quickly:

"I've seen you play at Wimbledon, sir."

Nevile half turned his head.

"Oh, yes, have you?"

He was throwing aside some of the rackets. There were two golf bags in the cupboard leaning up against fishing tackle.

"Only my wife and I play golf," explained Nevile. "And that's a man's club. Yes, that's right—it's mine."

He had taken out his bag which contained at least fourteen clubs.

Inspector Leach thought to himself:

"These athletic chaps certainly take themselves seriously. Wouldn't like to be his caddy."

Nevile was saying:

"It's one of Walter Hudson's niblicks from St. Esbert's."

"Thank you, Mr. Strange. That settles one question."

Nevile said:

"What beats me is that nothing was taken. And the house doesn't seem to have been broken into?" His voice was bewildered—but it was also frightened.

Battle said to himself:

"They've been thinking it out, all of them. . . ."

"The servants," said Nevile, "are so absolutely harmless."

"I shall talk to Miss Alden about the servants," said

Inspector Leach smoothly. "In the meantime I wonder if you could give me any idea who Lady Tressilian's solicitors are?"

"Askwith & Trelawny," replied Nevile promptly. "St. Loo."

"Thank you, Mr. Strange. We shall have to find out from them all about Lady Tressilian's property."

"Do you mean," asked Nevile, "who inherits her money?"

"That's right, sir. Her will, and all that."

"I don't know about her will," said Nevile. "She had not very much of her own to leave so far as I know. I can tell you about the bulk of her property."

"Yes, Mr. Strange?"

"It comes to me and my wife under the will of the late Sir Matthew Tressilian. Lady Tressilian only had a life interest in it."

"Indeed, is that so?" Inspector Leach looked at Nevile with the interested attention of someone who spots a possibly valuable addition to his pet collection. The look made Nevile wince nervously. Inspector Leach went on and his voice was impossibly genial, "You've no idea of the amount, Mr. Strange?"

"I couldn't tell you off hand. In the neighborhood of a hundred thousand pounds, I believe."

"In-deed. To each of you?"

"No, divided between us."

"I see. A very considerable sum."

Nevile smiled. He said quietly, "I've got plenty to live on of my own, you know, without hankering to step into dead people's shoes."

Inspector Leach looked shocked at having such ideas attributed to him.

They went back into the dining room and Leach said his next little piece. This was on the subject of fingerprints—a matter of routine—elimination of those of the household in the dead woman's bedroom.

Everyone expressed willingness—almost eagerness—to have their fingerprints taken.

They were shepherded into the library for that purpose where Detective Sergeant Jones was waiting for them with his little roller.

Battle and Leach began on the servants.

Nothing very much was to be got from them. Hurstall explained his system of locking up the house and swore that he had found it untouched in the morning. There were no signs of any entry by an intruder. The front door, he explained, had been left on the latch. That is to say it was not bolted, but could be opened from outside with a key. It was left like that because Mr. Nevile had gone over to Easterhead Bay and would be back late.

"Do you know what time he came in?"

"Yes, sir, I think it was about half past two. Someone came back with him, I think. I heard voices and then a car drive away and then I heard the door close and Mr. Nevile come upstairs."

"What time did he leave here last night for Easterhead Bay?"

"About twenty past ten. I heard the door close."

Leach nodded. There did not seem much more to be got from Hurstall at the moment. He interviewed the others. They were all disposed to be nervous and frightened, but no more so than was natural in the circumstances.

Leach looked questioningly at his uncle as the door closed behind the slightly hysterical kitchenmaid who had tailed the procession.

Battle said: "Have the housemaid back—not the pop-eyed one—the tall thin bit of vinegar. She knows something."

Emma Wales was clearly uneasy. It alarmed her that this time it was the big elderly square man who took upon himself the task of questioning her.

"I'm just going to give you a bit of advice, Miss Wales," he said pleasantly. "It doesn't do, you know, to hold anything back from the police. Makes them look at you unfavorably, if you understand what I mean——"

Emma Wales protested indignantly but uneasily:

"I'm sure I never——"

"Now, now." Battle held up a large square hand. "You saw something or else you heard something—— what was it?"

"I didn't exactly hear it—I mean I couldn't help hearing it—Mr. Hurstall, he heard it too. And I don't think, not for a moment I don't, that it had anything to do with the murder."

"Probably not, probably not. Just tell us what it was."

"Well, I was going up to bed. Just after ten it was—— and I'd slipped along first to put Miss Aldin's hot water bottle in her bed. Summer or winter she always has one, and so of course I had to pass right by her ladyship's door."

"Go on," said Battle.

"And I heard her and Mr. Nevile going at it hammer and tongs. Voices right up. Shouting, he was. Oh, it was a proper quarrel!"

"Remember exactly what was said?"

"Well, I wasn't really listening as you might say."

"No. But still you must have heard some of the words."

"Her ladyship was saying as she wouldn't have something or other going on in her house and Mr. Nevile was saying, 'Don't you dare to say anything against her.' All worked up he was."

Battle, with an expressionless face, tried once more,

but he could get no more out of her. In the end he dismissed the woman.

He and Jim looked at each other. Leach said, after a minute or two:

"Jones ought to be able to tell us something about those prints by now."

Battle asked:

"Who's doing the rooms?"

"Williams. He's a good man. He won't miss anything."

"You're keeping the occupants out of them?"

"Yes. Until Williams has finished."

The door opened at that minute and young Williams put his head in.

"There's something I'd like you to see. In Mr. Nevile Strange's room."

They got up and followed him to the suite on the west side of the house.

Williams pointed to a heap on the floor. A dark blue coat, trousers and waistcoat.

Leach said sharply:

"Where did you find this?"

"Bundled down into the bottom of the wardrobe. Just look at *this,* sir."

He picked up the coat and showed the edges of the dark blue cuffs.

"See those dark stains? That's blood, sir, or I'm a Dutchman. And see here, it's spattered all up the sleeve."

"Hm," Battle avoided the other's eager eyes. "Looks bad for young Nevile, I must say. Any other suit in the room?"

"Dark grey pin stripe hanging over a chair. Lot of water on the floor here by the wash basin."

"Looking as though he washed the blood off himself in the devil of a hurry? Yes. It's near the open window, though, and the rain has come in a good deal."

"Not enough to make those pools on the floor, sir. They're not dried up yet."

Battle was silent. A picture was forming itself before his eyes. A man with blood on his hands and sleeves, flinging off his clothes, bundling the bloodstained garments into the cupboard, sluicing water furiously over his hands and bare arms.

He looked across at a door in the other wall.

Williams answered the look.

"Mrs. Strange's room, sir. The door is locked."

"Locked? On this side?"

"No. On the other."

"On her side, eh?"

Battle was reflective for a minute or two. He said at last, "Let's see that old butler again."

Hurstall was nervous. Leach said crisply:

"Why didn't you tell us, Hurstall, that you overheard a quarrel between Mr. Strange and Lady Tressilian last night?"

The old man blinked.

"I really didn't think twice about it, sir. I don't imagine it was what you'd call a quarrel—just an amicable difference of opinion."

Resisting the temptation to say, "Amicable difference of opinion my foot!" Leach went on:

"What suit was Mr. Strange wearing last night at dinner?"

Hurstall hesitated. Battle said quietly:

"Dark blue suit or grey pin stripe? I daresay someone else can tell us if you don't remember."

Hurstall broke his silence.

"I remember now, sir. It was his dark blue. The family," he added, anxious not to lose prestige, "have not been in the habit of changing into evening dress during the summer months. They frequently go out after dinner—sometimes in the garden, sometimes down to the quay."

Battle nodded. Hurstall left the room. He passed Jones in the doorway. Jones looked excited.

He said:

"It's a cinch, sir. I've got all their prints. There's only one fits the bill. Of course I've only been able to make a rough comparison as yet, but I'll bet they're the right ones."

"Well?" said Battle.

"The prints on that niblick handle, sir, *were made by Mr. Nevile Strange.*"

Battle leant back in his chair.

"Well," he said, "that seems to settle it, doesn't it?"

## IV

THEY WERE in the Chief Constable's office—three men with grave worried faces.

Major Mitchell said with a sigh:

"Well, I suppose there's nothing to be done but arrest him?"

Leach said quietly:

"Looks like it, sir."

Mitchell looked across at Superintendent Battle.

"Cheer up, Battle," he said kindly. "Your best friend isn't dead."

Superintendent Battle sighed.

"I don't like it," he said.

"I don't think any of us like it," said Mitchell. "But we've ample evidence, I think, to apply for a warrant."

"More than ample," said Battle.

"In fact if we don't apply for one, anybody might ask why the dickens not?"

Battle nodded an unhappy head.

"Let's go over it," said the Chief Constable. "You've got motive—Strange and his wife come into a considerable sum of money at the old lady's death. He's the last person known to have seen her alive—he was heard quarreling with her. The suit he wore that night had bloodstains on it—and that blood is the same group as that of the deceased woman (that's only negative evidence, of course); most damning of all, his fingerprints were found upon the actual weapon—*and no one else's.*"

"And yet, sir," said Battle, *"you* don't like it either."

"I'm damned if I do."

"What is it exactly you don't like about it, sir?"

Major Mitchell rubbed his nose.

"Makes the fellow out a bit too much of a fool, perhaps?" he suggested.

"And yet, sir, they do behave like fools sometimes."

"Oh, I know—I know. Where would we be if they didn't?"

Battle said to Leach:

"What don't *you* like about it, Jim?"

Leach stirred unhappily.

"I've always liked Mr. Strange. Seen him on and off down here for years. He's a nice gentleman—and he's a sportsman."

"I don't see," said Battle slowly, "why a good tennis player shouldn't be a murderer as well. There's nothing against it." He paused. "What *I* don't like is the niblick."

"The niblick?" asked Mitchell, slightly puzzled.

"Yes, sir, or alternatively, the bell. The bell or the niblick—not both."

He went on in his slow careful voice.

"What do we think actually happened? Did Mr. Strange go to her room, have a quarrel, lose his temper, and hit her over the head with a niblick? If so, and it was unpremeditated, how did he happen to have a niblick with him? It's not the sort of thing you carry about with you in the evenings."

"He might have been practicing swings—something like that."

"He might—but nobody says so. Nobody saw him doing it. The last time anybody saw him with a niblick in his hand was about a week previously when he was practicing sand shots down on the sands. As I look at it, you see, you can't have it both ways. Either there was a quarrel and he lost his temper—and mind you, I've seen him on the courts, and in one of these tournament matches these tennis stars are all het up and a mass of nerves and if their tempers fray easily it's going to show. I've never seen Mr. Strange ruffled. I should say he'd got an excellent control over his temper—better than most—and yet we're suggesting that he goes berserk and hits a frail old lady over the head."

"There's another alternative, Battle," said the Chief Constable.

"I know, sir. The theory that it was premeditated. He wanted the old lady's money. That fits in with the bell—which entailed the doping of the maid—but it *doesn't* fit in with the niblick and the quarrel! If he'd made up his mind to do her in, he'd be very careful *not* to quarrel with her. He could dope the maid—creep into her room in the night—crack her over the head and stage a nice little robbery, wiping the niblick and putting it carefully back where it belonged! It's all wrong, sir—it's a mixture of cold premeditation and unpremeditated violence—and the two don't mix!"

"There's something in what you say, Battle—but—what's the alternative?"

"It's the niblick that takes my fancy, sir."

"Nobody could have hit her over the head with that niblick without disturbing Nevile's prints—that's quite certain."

"In that case," said Superintendent Battle, "she was hit over the head with something else."

Major Mitchell drew a deep breath.

"That's rather a wild assumption, isn't it?"

"I think it's common sense, sir. Either Strange hit her with that niblick or nobody did. I plump for nobody. In that case that niblick was put there deliberately and blood and hair smeared on it. Dr. Lazenby doesn't like the niblick much—he had to accept it because it was the obvious thing and because he couldn't say definitely that it *hadn't* been used."

Major Mitchell leaned back in his chair.

"Go on, Battle," he said. "I'm giving you a free hand. What's the next step?"

"Take away the niblick," said Battle, "and what is left? First, motive. Had Nevile Strange really got a motive for doing away with Lady Tressilian? He inherited money—a lot depends to my mind on whether he needed that money. He says not. I'd suggest we verify that. Find out the state of his finances. If he's in a hole financially, and needs money, then the case against him is very much strengthened. If, on the other hand, he was speaking the truth and his finances are in a good state, why, then—"

"Well, what then?"

"Why, then we might have a look at the motives of the other people in the house."

"You think, then, that Nevile Strange was framed?"

Superintendent Battle screwed up his eyes.

"There's a phrase I read somewhere that tickled my fancy. Something about a fine Italian hand. That's what I seem to see in this business. Ostensibly it's a blunt brutal straightforward crime, but it seems to me I catch glimpses of something else—of a fine Italian hand at work behind the scenes. . . ."

There was a long pause while the Chief Constable looked at Battle.

"You may be right," he said at last. "Dash it all, there's something funny about the business. What's your idea, now, of our plan of campaign?"

Battle stroked his square jaw.

"Well, sir," he said. "I'm always in favor of going about things in the obvious way. Everything's been set to make us suspicious of Mr. Nevile Strange. Let's go on being suspicious of him. Needn't go so far as actually to arrest him, but hint at it, question him, put the wind up him—and observe everybody's reactions generally. Verify his statements, go over his movements that night with a toothcomb. In fact show our hand as plainly as may be."

"Quite Machiavellian," said Major Mitchell with a twinkle. "Imitation of a heavy-handed policeman by star actor Battle."

The Superintendent smiled.

"I always like doing what's expected of me, sir. This time I mean to be a bit slow about it—take my time. I want to do some nosing about. Being suspicious of Mr. Nevile Strange is a very good excuse for nosing about. I've an idea, you know, that something rather odd has been going on in that house."

"Looking for the sex angle?"

"If you like to put it that way, sir."

"Handle it your own way, Battle. You and Leach carry on between you."

"Thank you, sir." Battle stood up. "Nothing suggestive from the solicitors?"

"No, I rang them up. I know Trelawny fairly well. He's sending me a copy of Sir Matthew's will and also of Lady Tressilian's. She had about five hundred a year of her own—invested in gilt-edged securities. She left a legacy to Barrett and a small one to Hurstall, the rest to Mary Aldin."

"That's three we might keep an eye on," said Battle.

Mitchell looked amused.

"Suspicious fellow, aren't you?"

"No use letting oneself be hypnotized by fifty thousand pounds," said Battle stolidly. "Many a murder has been done for less than fifty pounds. It depends on how much you want the money. Barrett got a legacy—and maybe she took the precaution to dope herself so as to avert suspicion."

"She very nearly passed out. Lazenby hasn't let us question her yet."

"Overdid it out of ignorance, perhaps. Then Hurstall may have been in bad need of cash for all we know. And Miss Aldin, if she's no money of her own, might have fancied a bit of life on a nice little income before she's too old to enjoy it."

The Chief Constable looked doubtful.

"Well," he said, "it's up to you two. Get on with the job."


V


BACK AT Gull's Point, the two police officers received Williams' report.

Nothing of a suspicious or suggestive nature had been found in any of the bedrooms. The servants were clamoring to be allowed to get on with the housework. Should he give them the word?

"Might as well, I suppose," said Battle. "I'll just have a stroll myself first through the upper floors. Rooms that haven't been done very often tell you something about their occupants that's useful to know."

Jones put down a small cardboard box on the table.

"From Mr. Nevile Strange's dark blue coat," he announced. "The red hairs were on the cuff, blonde hairs on the inside of the collar and the right shoulder."

Battle took out the two long red hairs and the half dozen blonde ones and looked at them. He said, with a faint twinkle in his eye:

"Convenient. One blonde, one redhead and one brunette in this house. So we know where we are at once. Red hair on the cuff, blonde on the collar? Mr. Nevile Strange does seem to be a bit of a Bluebeard. His arm round one wife and the other one's head on his shoulder."

"The blood on the sleeve has gone for analysis, sir. They'll ring us up as soon as they get the result."

Leach nodded.

"What about the servants?"

"I followed your instructions, sir. None of them is under notice to leave, or seems likely to have borne a grudge against the old lady. She was strict, but well liked. In any case the management of the servants lay with Miss Aldin. She seems to have been popular with them."

"Thought she was an efficient woman the moment I laid eyes on her," said Battle. "If she's our murderess, she won't be easy to hang."

Jones looked startled.

"But those prints on that niblick, sir, were——"

"I know—I know," said Battle. "The singularly obliging Mr. Strange's. There's a general belief that athletes aren't overburdened by brains (not at all true, by the way) but I can't believe Nevile Strange is a complete moron. What about those senna pods of the maid's?"

"They were always on the shelf in the servants' bathroom on the second floor. She used to put 'em in to soak midday and they stood there until the evening when she went to bed."

"So that absolutely anybody could get at them? Anybody inside the house, that is to say."

Leach said with conviction:

"It's an inside job all right!"

"Yes, I think so. Not that this is one of those closed-circle crimes. It isn't. Anyone who had a key could have opened the front door and walked in. Nevile Strange had that key last night—but it would probably be a simple matter to have got one cut, or an old hand could do it with a bit of wire. But I don't see any outsider knowing about the bell and that Barrett took senna at night! That's local inside knowledge! Come along, Jim, my boy. Let's go up and see this bathroom and all the rest of it."

They started on the top floor. Here was a box room full of old broken furniture and junk of all kinds.

"I haven't looked through this, sir," said Jones. "I didn't know—"

"What you were looking for? Quite right. Only waste of time. From the dust on the floor nobody has been in here for at least six months."

The servants' rooms were all on this floor, also two unoccupied bedrooms with a bathroom, and Battle looked into each room and gave it a cursory glance noticing that Alice, the popeyed housemaid, slept with her window shut; that Emma, the thin one, had a great many relations, photographs of whom were crowded on her chest of drawers, and that Hurstall had one or two pieces of good, though cracked, Dresden and Crown Derby porcelain.

The cook's room was severely neat and the kitchenmaid's chaotically untidy. Battle passed on into the bathroom which was the room nearest to the head of the stairs. Williams pointed out the long shelf over the washbasin, on which stood tooth glasses and brushes, various unguents and bottles of salts and hair lotion. A packet of senna pod stood open at one end.

"No prints on the glass or packet?"

"Only the maid's own. I got hers from her room."

"He didn't need to handle the glass," said Leach. He'd only have to drop the stuff in."

Battle went down the stairs followed by Leach. Halfway down this top flight was a rather awkwardly placed window. A pole with a hook on the end stood in a corner.

"You draw down the top sash with that," explained Leach. "But there's a burglar screw. The window can be drawn down, only so far. Too narrow for anyone to get in that way."

"I wasn't thinking of anyone getting in," said Battle. His eyes were thoughtful.

He went into the first bedroom on the next floor which was Audrey Strange's. It was neat and fresh, ivory brushes on the dressing table—no clothes lying about. Battle looked into the wardrobe. Two plain coats and skirts, a couple of evening dresses, one or two summer frocks. The dresses were cheap, the tailormades well cut and expensive but not new.

Battle nodded. He stood at the writing table a minute or two, fiddling with the pen tray on the left of the blotter.

Williams said: "Nothing of any interest on the blotting paper or in the waste paper basket."

"Your word's good enough," said Battle. "Nothing to be seen here."

They went on to the other rooms.

Thomas Royde's was untidy, with clothes lying about. Pipes and pipe ash on the tables and beside the bed, where a copy of Kipling's *Kim* lay half open.

"Used to native servants clearing up after him," said Battle. "Likes reading old favorites. Conservative type."

Mary Aldin's room was small but comfortable. Battle looked at the travel books on the shelves and the old-fashioned dented silver brushes. The furnishing and coloring in the room were more modern than the rest of the house.

"She's not so conservative," said Battle. "No photographs either. Not one who lives in the past."

There were three or four empty rooms, all well kept and dusted ready for occupation, and a couple of bathrooms. Then came Lady Tressilian's big double room. After that, reached by going down three little steps, came the two rooms and bathroom occupied by the Stranges.

Battle did not waste much time in Nevile's room. He glanced out of the open casement window below which the rocks fell sheer to the sea. The view was to the west, towards Stark Head which rose wild and forbidding out of the sea.

"Gets the afternoon sun," he murmured. "But rather a grim morning outlook. Nasty smell of seaweed at low tide, too. And that headland has got a grim look. Don't wonder it attracts suicides!"

He passed into the larger room, the door of which had been unlocked.

Here everything was in wild confusion. Clothes lay about in heaps—filmy underwear, stockings, jumpers tried on and discarded—a patterned summer frock thrown sprawling over the back of a chair. Battle looked inside the wardrobe. It was full of furs, evening dresses, shorts, tennis frocks, playsuits.

Battle shut the doors again almost reverently.

"Expensive tastes," he remarked. "She must cost her husband a lot of money."

Leach said darkly:

"Perhaps that's why——"

He left the sentence unfinished.

"Why he needed a hundred—or rather fifty thousand pounds? Maybe. We'd better see, I think, what he has to say about it."

They went down to the library. Williams was dispatched to tell the servants they could get on with the housework. The family were free to return to their rooms if they wished. They were to be informed of that fact and also that Inspector Leach would like an interview with each of them separately starting with Mr. Nevile Strange.

When Williams had gone out of the room, Battle and Leach established themselves behind a massive Victorian table. A young policeman with notebook sat in the corner of the room, his pencil poised.

Battle said:

"You carry on for a start, Jim. Make it impressive." As the other nodded his head, Battle rubbed his chin and frowned.

"I wish I knew what keeps putting Hercule Poirot into my head."

"You mean that old chap—the Belgian—comic little guy?"

"Comic my foot," said Superintendent Battle. "About as dangerous as a black mamba and a she-leopard— that's what *he* is when he starts making a mountebank of himself! I wish he were here—this sort of thing would be right up his street."

"In what way?"

"Psychology," said Battle. "Real psychology—not the half-baked stuff people hand out who know nothing about it." His memory dwelt resentfully on Miss Amphrey and his daughter, Sylvia. "No—the real genuine article—knowing just what makes the wheels go round. Keep a murderer talking—that's one of his lines. Says everyone is bound to speak what's true sooner or later —because in the end it's easier than telling lies. And so they make some little slip they don't think matters—and that's when you get them."

"So you're going to give Nevile Strange plenty of rope?"

Battle gave an absent-minded assent. Then he added, in some annoyance and perplexity:

"But what's really worrying me is—what put Hercule Poirot into my head? Upstairs—that's where it was. Now what did I see that reminded me of that little guy?"

The conversation was put to an end by the arrival of Nevile Strange.

He looked pale and worried, but much less nervous than he had done at the breakfast table. Battle eyed him keenly. Incredible that a man who knew—and he must know if he were capable of any thought processes at all—that he had left his fingerprints on the instrument of the crime—and who had since had his fingerprints taken by the police—should show neither intense nervousness nor an elaborate brazening of it out.

Nevile Strange looked quite natural—shocked, worried, grieved—and just slightly and healthily nervous.

Jim Leach was speaking in his pleasant West country voice.

"We would like you to answer certain questions, Mr. Strange. Both as to your movements last night and in reference to particular facts. At the same time I must caution you that you are not bound to answer these questions unless you like and that if you prefer to do so you may have your solicitor present."

He leaned back to observe the effect of this.

Nevile Strange looked, quite plainly, bewildered.

"He hasn't the least idea what we're getting at, or else he's a damned good actor," Leach thought to himself. Aloud he said, as Nevile did not answer, "Well, Mr. Strange?"

Nevile said:

"Of course, ask me anything you like."

"You realize," said Battle pleasantly, "that anything you say will be taken down in writing and may subsequently be used in a court of law in evidence."

A flash of temper showed on Strange's face. He said sharply:

"Are you threatening me?"

"No, no, Mr. Strange. Warning you."

Nevile shrugged his shoulders.

"I suppose all this is part of your routine. Go ahead."

"You are ready to make a statement?"

"If that's what you call it."

"Then will you tell us exactly what you did last night. From dinner onwards, shall we say?"

"Certainly. After dinner we went into the drawing room. We had coffee. We listened to the wireless—the news and so on. Then I decided to go across to Easterhead Bay Hotel and look up a chap who is staying there —a friend of mind."

"That friend's name is?"

"Latimer. Edward Latimer."

"An intimate friend?"

"Oh, so, so. We've seen a good deal of him since he's been down here. He's been over to lunch and dinner and we've been over there."

Battle said:

"Rather late, wasn't it, to go off to Easterhead Bay?"

"Oh, it's a gay spot—they keep it up till all hours."

"But this is rather an early to bed household, isn't it?"

"Yes, on the whole. However, I took the latchkey with me. Nobody had to sit up."

"Your wife didn't think of going with you?"

There was a slight change, a stiffening in Nevile's tone as he said:

"No, she had a headache. She'd already gone up to bed."

"Please go on, Mr. Strange."

"I was just going up to change."

Leach interrupted.

"Excuse me, Mr. Strange. Change into what? Into evening dress or out of evening dress?"

"Neither. I was wearing a blue suit—my best, as it happened, and as it was raining a bit and I proposed to take the ferry and walk the other side—it's about half a mile, as you know—I changed into an older suit—a grey pin stripe if you want me to go into every detail."

"We do like to get things clear," said Leach humbly. "Please go on."

"I was going upstairs, as I say, when Hurstall came and told me Lady Tressilian wanted to see me, so I went along and had a—a jaw with her for a bit."

Battle said gently:

"You were the last person to see her alive, I think, Mr. Strange?"

Nevile flushed.

"Yes—yes—I suppose I was. She was quite all right then."

"How long were you with her?"

"About twenty minutes to half an hour, I should think, then I went to my room, changed my suit and hurried off. I took the latchkey with me."

"What time was that?"

"About half past ten, I should think. I hurried down the hill, just caught the ferry starting and went on as planned. I found Latimer at the Hotel, we had a drink or two and a game of billiards. The time passed so quickly that I found I'd lost the last ferry back. It goes at one thirty. So Latimer very decently got out his car and drove me back. That, as you know, means going all the way round by Saltington—sixteen miles. We left the

Hotel at two o'clock and got back here somewhere around half past, I should say. I thanked Ted Latimer, asked him in for a drink, but he said he'd rather get straight back, so I let myself in and went straight up to bed. I didn't hear or see anything amiss. The house seemed all asleep and peaceful. Then this morning I heard that girl screaming and——"

Leach stopped him.

"Quite, quite. Now to go back a little—to your conversation with Lady Tressilian—she was quite normal in her manner?"

"Oh, absolutely."

"What did you talk about?"

"Oh, one thing and another."

"Amicably?"

Nevile flushed.

"Certainly."

"You didn't, for instance," went on Leach smoothly, "have a violent quarrel?"

Nevile did not answer at once. Leach said:

"You had better tell the truth, you know. I'll tell you frankly some of your conversation was overheard."

Nevile said shortly:

"We had a bit of a disagreement. It was nothing."

"What was the subject of the disagreement?"

With an effort Nevile recovered his temper. He smiled.

"Frankly," he said, "she ticked me off. That often happened. If she disapproved of anyone she let them have it straight from the shoulder. She was old-fashioned, you see, and she was inclined to be down on modern ways and modern lines of thought—divorce—all that. We had an argument and I may have got a bit heated, but we parted on perfectly friendly terms—agreeing to differ." He added, with some heat, "I certainly didn't bash her over the head because I lost my temper over an argument—if that's what you think!"

Leach glanced at Battle. Battle leaned forward ponderously across the table. He said:

"You recognized that niblick as your property this morning. Have you any explanation for the fact that your fingerprints were found upon it?"

Nevile stared. He said sharply:

"I—but of course they would be—it's my club—I've often handled it."

"Any explanation, I mean, for the fact that your fingerprints show that *you were the last person to have handled it.*"

Nevile sat quite still. The color had gone out of his face.

"That's not true," he said at last. "It can't be. Somebody could have handled it after me—someone wearing gloves."

"No, Mr. Strange—nobody could have handled it *in the sense you mean*—by raising it to strike—without blurring your own marks."

There was a pause—a very long pause.

"Oh, God," said Nevile convulsively and gave a long shudder. He put his hands over his eyes. The two policemen watched him.

Then he took away his hands. He sat up straight.

"It isn't true," he said quietly. "It simply isn't true. You think I killed her, but I didn't. I swear I didn't. There's some horrible mistake."

"You've no explanation to offer about those fingerprints?"

"How can I have? I'm dumfounded."

"Have you any explanation for the fact that the sleeves and cuffs of your dark blue suit are stained with blood?"

"Blood?" It was a horror-struck whisper. "It couldn't be!"

"You didn't, for instance, cut yourself—"

"No. No, of course I didn't!"

They waited a little while.

Nevile Strange, his forehead creased, seemed to be thinking. He looked up at them at last with frightened horror-stricken eyes.

"It's fantastic!" he said. "Simply fantastic. It's none of it *true*."

"Facts are true enough," said Superintendent Battle.

"But why should I do such a thing. It's unthinkable —unbelievable! I've known Camilla all my life."

Leach coughed.

"I believe you told us yourself, Mr. Strange, that you come into a good deal of money upon Lady Tressilian's death?"

"You think that's why— But I don't want money! I don't *need* it!"

"That," said Leach, with his little cough, "is what you *say*, Mr. Strange."

Nevile sprang up.

"Look here, that's something I *can* prove. That I didn't need money. Let me ring up my bank manager —you can talk to him yourself."

The call was put through. The line was clear and in a very few minutes they were through to London. Nevile spoke:

"That you, Ronaldson? Nevile Strange speaking. You know my voice. Look here, will you give the police— they're here now—all the information they want about my affairs— Yes— Yes, please."

Leach took the phone. He spoke quietly. It went on, question and answer.

He replaced the phone at last.

"Well," said Nevile eagerly.

Leach said impassively, "You have a substantial credit balance, and the bank has charge of all your investments and reports them to be in a favorable condition."

"So you see it's true what I said!"

"It seems so—but again, Mr. Strange, you may have commitments, debts—payment of blackmail—reasons for requiring money of which we do not know."

"But I haven't! I assure you I haven't. You won't find anything of that kind."

Superintendent Battle shifted his heavy shoulders. He spoke in a kind fatherly voice.

"We've sufficient evidence, as I'm sure you'll agree, Mr. Strange, to ask for a warrant for your arrest. We haven't done so—*as yet!* We're giving you the benefit of the doubt, you see."

Nevile said bitterly:

"You mean, don't you, that you've made up your minds I did it, but you want to get at the motive so as to clinch the case against me?"

Battle was silent. Leach looked at the ceiling.

Nevile said desperately:

"It's like some awful dream. There's nothing I can say or do. It's like being in a trap and you can't get out."

Superintendent Battle stirred. An intelligent gleam showed between his half-closed lids.

"That's very nicely put," he said. "Very nicely put indeed. It gives me an idea. . . ."


## VI


Sergeant Jones adroitly got rid of Nevile through the hall and dining room and then brought Kay in by the French window so that husband and wife did not meet.

"He'll see all the others, though," Leach remarked.

"All the better," said Battle. "It's only this one I want to deal with whilst she's still in the dark."

The day was overcast with a sharp wind. Kay was dressed in a tweed skirt and a purple sweater above which her hair looked like a burnished copper bowl. She looked half frightened, half excited. Her beauty and vitality bloomed against the dark Victorian background of books and saddleback chairs.

Leach led her easily enough over her account of the previous evening.

She had had a headache and gone to bed early— about quarter past nine, she thought. She had slept heavily and heard nothing until the next morning when she was wakened by hearing someone screaming.

Battle took up the questioning.

"Your husband didn't come in to see how you were before he went off for the evening?"

"No."

"You didn't see him from the time you left the drawing room until the following morning. Is that right?"

Kay nodded.

Battle stroked his jaw.

"Mrs. Strange, the door between your room and that of your husband was locked. Who locked it?"

Kay said shortly: "I did."

Battle said nothing—but he waited—waited like an elderly fatherly cat—for a mouse to come out of the hole he was watching.

His silence did what questions might not have accomplished. Kay burst out impetuously:

"Oh, I suppose you've got to have it all! That old doddering Hurstall must have heard us before tea and he'll tell you if I don't. He's probably told you already. Nevile and I had had a row—a flaming row! I was furious with him! I went up to bed and locked the door because I was still in a flaming rage with him!"

"I see—I see," said Battle at his most sympathetic. "And what was the trouble all about?"

"Does it matter? Oh, I don't mind telling you. Nevile has been behaving like a perfect idiot. It's all that woman's fault, though."

"What woman?"

"His first wife. She got him to come here in the first place."

"You mean—to meet you?"

"Yes. Nevile thinks it was all his own idea—poor innocent! But it wasn't. He never thought of such a thing until he met her in the Park one day and she got the idea into his head and made him believe he'd thought of it himself. He quite honestly thinks it was his idea, but I've seen Audrey's fine Italian hand behind it from the first."

"Why should she do such a thing?" asked Battle.

"Because she wanted to get hold of him again," said Kay. She spoke quickly and her breath came fast. "She's never forgiven him for going off with me. This is her revenge. She got him to fix up that we'd all be here together and then she got to work on him. She's been doing it ever since we arrived. She's clever, you know. Knows just how to look pathetic and elusive— yes, and how to play up another man, too. She got Thomas Royde, a faithful old dog who's always adored her, to be here at the same time, and she drove Nevile mad by pretending she was going to marry him."

She stopped, breathing angrily.

Battle said mildly:

"I should have thought he'd be glad for her to—er— find happiness with an old friend."

"Glad? He's jealous as hell!"

"Then he must be very fond of her."

"Oh, he is," said Kay bitterly. *"She's* seen to that!"

Battle's finger still ran dubiously over his jaw.

"You might have objected to this arrangement of coming here?" he suggested.

"How could I? It would have looked as though I were jealous!"

"Well," said Battle, "after all, you were, weren't you?"

Kay flushed.

"Always! I've always been jealous of Audrey. Right from the beginning—or nearly the beginning. I used to feel her there in the house. It was, as though it were *her* house, not mine. I changed the color scheme and did it all up but it was no good! I'd feel her there like a grey ghost creeping about. I knew Nevile worried because he thought he'd treated her badly. He couldn't quite forget about her—she was always there—a reproachful feeling at the back of his mind. There are people, you know, who are like that. They seem rather colorless and not very interesting—but they make themselves *felt*."

Battle nodded thoughtfully. He said:

"Well, thank you, Mrs. Strange. That's all at present. We have to ask—er—a good many questions—especially with your husband inheriting so much money from Lady Tressilian—fifty thousand pounds—"

"Is it as much as that? We get it from old Sir Matthew's will, don't we?"

"You know all about it?"

"Oh, yes. He left it to be divided between Nevile and Nevile's wife. Not that I'm glad the old thing is dead. I'm not. I didn't like her very much—probably because she didn't like me—but it's too horrible to think of some burglar coming along and cracking her head open."

She went out on that. Battle looked at Leach.

"What do you think of her? Good-looking bit of

goods, I will say. A man could lose his head over her easy enough."

Leach agreed.

"Doesn't seem to be quite a lady, though," he said dubiously.

"They aren't nowadays," said Battle. "Shall we see No. 1? No, I think we'll have Miss Aldin next, and get an outside angle on this matrimonial business."

Mary Aldin came in composedly and sat down. Beneath her outward calmness her eyes looked worried.

She answered Leach's questions clearly enough, confirming Nevile's account of the evening. She had come up to bed about ten o'clock.

"Mr. Strange was then with Lady Tressilian?"

"Yes, I could hear them talking."

"Talking, Miss Aldin, or quarreling?"

She flushed but answered quietly:

"Lady Tressilian, you know, was fond of discussion. She often sounded acrimonious when she was really nothing of the kind. Also, she was inclined to be autocratic and to domineer over people—and a man doesn't take that kind of thing as easily as a woman does."

"As you do, perhaps," thought Battle.

He looked at her intelligent face. It was she who broke the silence.

"I don't want to be stupid—but it really seems to me incredible—quite incredible, that you should suspect one of the people in this house. Why shouldn't it be an outsider?"

"For several reasons, Miss Aldin. For one thing, nothing was taken and no entry was forced. I needn't remind you of the geography of your own house and grounds, but just bear this in mind. On the west is a sheer cliff down to the sea, to the south are a couple of terraces with a wall and a drop to the sea, on the east the garden slopes down almost to the shore, but it is surrounded by a high wall. The only ways out are a small door leading through on to the road which was found bolted inside as usual this morning and the main door to the house which is set on the road. I'm not saying no one could climb that wall, nor that they could not have got in by using a spare key to the front door or even a skeleton key—but I'm saying that as far as I can see no one did do anything of the sort. Whoever committed this crime knew that Barrett took senna pod infusion every night and doped it—that means someone in the house. The niblick was taken from the cupboard under the stairs. *It wasn't an outsider, Miss Aldin.*"

"It wasn't Nevile! I'm sure it wasn't Nevile!"

"Why are you so sure?"

She raised her hands hopelessly.

"It just isn't like him—that's why! He wouldn't kill a defenseless old woman in bed—*Nevile!*"

"It doesn't seem very likely," said Battle reasonably, "but you'd be surprised at the things people do when they've got a good enough reason. Mr. Strange may have wanted money very badly."

"I'm sure he didn't. He's not an extravagant person —he never has been."

"No, but his wife is."

"Kay? Yes, perhaps—but, oh, it's too ridiculous. I'm sure the last thing Nevile has been thinking of lately is money."

Superintendent Battle coughed.

"He's had other worries, I understand?"

"Kay told you, I suppose? Yes, it really has been rather difficult. Still, it's nothing to do with this dreadful business."

"Probably not, but all the same I'd like to hear your version of the affair, Miss Aldin."

Mary said slowly:

"Well, as I say, it has created a difficult—situation. Whoever's idea it was to begin with—"

He interrupted her deftly.

"I understood it was Mr. Nevile Strange's idea?"

"He said it was."

"But you yourself didn't think so?"

"I—no—it isn't like Nevile somehow. I've had a feeling all along that somebody else put the idea into his head."

"Mrs. Audrey Strange, perhaps?"

"It seems incredible that Audrey should do such a thing."

"Then who else could it have been?"

Mary raised her shoulders helplessly.

"I don't know. It's just—queer."

"Queer," said Battle thoughtfully. "That's what I feel about this case. It's queer."

"Everything's been queer. There's been a feeling—I can't describe it. Something in the air. A *menace*."

"Everybody strung up and on edge?"

"Yes, just that. . . . We've all suffered from it. Even Mr. Latimer—" she stopped.

"I was just coming to Mr. Latimer. What can you tell me, Miss Aldin, about Mr. Latimer? Who is Mr. Latimer?"

"Well, really, I don't know much about him. He's a friend of Kay's."

"He's Mrs. Strange's friend? Known each other a long time?"

"Yes, she knew him before her marriage."

"Mr. Strange like him?"

"Quite well, I believe."

"No—trouble there?"

Battle put it delicately. Mary replied at once and emphatically:

"Certainly not!"

"Did Lady Tressilian like Mr. Latimer?"

"Not very much."

Battle took warning from the aloof tone of her voice and changed the subject.

"This maid, now, Jane Barrett, she has been with Lady Tressilian a long time? You consider her trustworthy?"

"Oh, absolutely. She was devoted to Lady Tressilian."

Battle leaned back in his chair.

"In fact you wouldn't consider for a moment the possibility that Barrett hit Lady Tressilian over the head and then doped herself to avoid being suspected?"

"Of course not. Why on earth should she?"

"She gets a legacy, you know."

"So do I," said Mary Aldin.

She looked at him steadily.

"Yes," said Battle. "So do you. Do you know how much?"

"Mr. Trelawny has just arrived. He told me."

"You didn't know about it beforehand?"

"No. I certainly assumed, from what Lady Tressilian occasionally let fall, that she had left me something. I have very little of my own, you know. Not enough to live on without getting work of some kind. I thought that Lady Tressilian would leave me at least a hundred a year—but she has some cousins and I did not at all know how she proposed to leave that money which was hers to dispose of. I knew, of course, that Sir Matthew's estate went to Nevile and Audrey."

"So she didn't know what Lady Tressilian was leaving her," Leach said when Mary Aldin had been dismissed. "At least that's what she *says*."

"That's what she says," agreed Battle. "And now for Bluebeard's first wife."

## VII

AUDREY WAS wearing a pale grey flannel coat and skirt. In it she looked so pale and ghostlike that Battle was reminded of Kay's words, "A grey ghost creeping about the house."

She answered his questions simply and without any signs of emotion.

Yes, she had gone to bed at ten o'clock, the same time as Miss Aldin. She had heard nothing during the night.

"You'll excuse me butting into your private affairs," said Battle, "but will you explain just how it comes about that you are here in the house?"

"I always come to stay at this time. This year, my—my late husband wanted to come at the same time and asked me if I would mind."

"It was his suggestion?"

"Oh, yes."

"Not yours?"

"Oh, no."

"But you agreed?"

"Yes, I agreed. . . . I didn't feel—that I could very well refuse."

"Why not, Mrs. Strange?"

But she was vague.

"One doesn't like to be disobliging."

"You were the injured party?"

"I beg your pardon?"

"It was you who divorced your husband?"

"Yes."

"Do you—excuse me—feel any rancor against him?"

"No—not at all."

"You have a very forgiving nature, Mrs. Strange."

She did not answer. He tried silence—but Audrey

was not Kay to be thus goaded into speech. She could remain silent without any hint of uneasiness. Battle acknowledged himself beaten.

"You are sure it was not your idea—this meeting?"

"Quite sure."

"You are on friendly terms with the present Mrs. Strange?"

"I don't think she likes me very much."

"Do you like her?"

"Yes. I think she is very beautiful."

"Well—thank you—I think that is all."

She got up and walked towards the door. Then she hesitated and came back.

"I would just like to say—" she spoke nervously and quickly. "You think Nevile did this—that he killed her because of the money. I'm quite sure that isn't so. Nevile has never cared much about money. I do know that. I was married to him for eight years, you know. I just can't see him killing anyone like that for money—it—it —isn't Nevile. I know my saying so isn't of any great value as evidence—but I do wish you would believe it."

She turned and hurried out of the room.

"And what do you make of *her?*" asked Leach. "I've never seen anyone so—so devoid of emotion."

"She didn't show any," said Battle. "But it's there. Some very strong emotion. *And I don't know what it is. . . .*"


## VIII

THOMAS ROYDE came last. He sat, solemn and stiff, blinking a little like an owl.

He was home from Malaya—first time for eight years. Had been in the habit of staying at Gull's Point ever since he was a boy. Mrs. Audrey Strange was a distant cousin—and had been brought up by his family from the age of nine. On the preceding night he had gone to bed just before eleven. Yes, he had heard Mr. Nevile Strange leave the house but had not seen him. Nevile had left at about twenty past ten or perhaps a little later. He himself had heard nothing during the night. He was up and in the garden when the discovery of Lady Tressilian's body had been made. He was an early riser.

There was a pause.

"Miss Aldin has told us that there was a state of tension in the house. Did you notice this too?"

"I don't think so. Don't notice things much."

"That's a lie," thought Battle to himself. "You notice a good deal, I should say—more than most."

No, he didn't think Nevile Strange had been short of money in any way. He certainly had not seemed so. But he knew very little about Mr. Strange's affairs.

"How well did you know the second Mrs. Strange?"

"I met her here for the first time."

Battle played his last card.

"You may know, Mr. Royde, that we've found Mr. Nevile Strange's fingerprints on the weapon. And we've found blood on the sleeve of the coat he wore last night."

He paused. Royde nodded.

"He was telling us," he muttered.

"I'm asking you frankly: *Do you think he did it?*"

Thomas Royde never liked to be hurried. He waited for a minute—which is a very long time—before he answered:

"Don't see why you ask *me?* Not my business. It's yours. Should say myself—very unlikely."

"Can you think of anyone who seems to you more likely?"

Thomas shook his head.

"Only person I think likely can't possibly have done it. So that's that."

"And who is that?"

But Royde shook his head more decidedly.

"Couldn't possibly say. Only my private opinion."

"It's your duty to assist the police."

"Tell you any facts. This isn't fact. Just idea. And it's impossible, anyway."

"We didn't get much out of him," said Leach when Royde had gone.

Battle agreed.

"No, we didn't. He's got something in his mind—something quite definite. I'd like to know what it is. This is a very peculiar sort of crime, Jim, my boy—"

The telephone rang before Leach could answer. He took up the receiver and spoke. After a minute or two of listening he said "Good," and slammed it down.

"Blood on the coat sleeve is human," he announced. "Same blood group as Lady T.'s. Looks as though Nevile Strange is in for it—"

Battle had walked over to the window and was looking out with considerable interest.

"A beautiful young man out there," he remarked. "Quite beautiful and a definite wrong 'un, I should say. It's a pity Mr. Latimer—for I feel that that's Mr. Latimer—was over at Easterhead Bay last night. He's the type that would smash in his own grandmother's head if he thought he could get away with it and if he knew he'd make something out of it."

"Well, there wasn't anything in it for him," said Leach. "Lady T.'s death doesn't benefit him in any way whatever." The telephone bell rang again. "Damn this phone, what's the matter now?"

He went to it.

"Hullo. Oh, it's you, Doctor? What? Come round, has she? What? *What?*"

He turned his head. "Uncle, just come and listen to this."

Battle came over and took the phone. He listened, his face as usual showing no expression. He said to Leach:

"Get Nevile Strange, Jim."

When Nevile came in, Battle was just replacing the phone on its hook.

Nevile, looking white and spent, stared curiously at the Scotland Yard Superintendent, trying to read the emotion behind the wooden mask.

"Mr. Strange," said Battle. "Do you know anyone who dislikes you very much?"

Nevile stared and shook his head.

"Sure?" Battle was impressive. "I mean, sir, someone who does more than dislike you—someone who—frankly—hates your guts?"

Nevile sat bolt upright.

"No. No, certainly not. Nothing of the kind."

"Think, Mr. Strange. Is there no one you've injured in any way—"

Nevile flushed.

"There's only one person I can be said to have injured and she's not the kind who bears rancor. That's my first wife when I left her for another woman. But I can assure you that she doesn't hate me. She's—she's been an angel."

The Superintendent leaned forward across the table.

"Let me tell you, Mr. Strange; you're a very lucky man. I don't say I liked the case against you—I didn't. But it *was* a case! It would have stood up all right, and unless the jury happened to have liked your personality, *it would have hanged you.*"

"You speak," said Nevile, "as though all that were past?"

"It is past," said Battle. "You've been saved, Mr. Strange, by pure chance."

Nevile still looked inquiringly at him.

"After you left her last night," said Battle, "Lady Tressilian rang the bell for her maid."

He watched whilst Nevile took it in.

"*After* . . . Then Barrett saw her—"

"Yes. *Alive and well*. Barrett also saw you leave the house before she went in to her mistress."

Nevile said:

"But the niblick—my fingerprints—"

"She wasn't hit with that niblick. Dr. Lazenby didn't like it at the time. I saw that. She was killed with something else. That niblick was put there deliberately to throw suspicion on *you*. It may be by someone who overheard the quarrel and so selected you as a suitable victim, or it may be because—"

He paused, and then repeated his question:

"Who is there in this house that hates you, Mr. Strange?"


## IX

"I've got a question for you, Doctor," said Battle.

They were in the doctor's house after returning from the nursing home where they had had a short interview with Jane Barrett.

Barrett was weak and exhausted but quite clear in her statement.

She had been just getting into bed after drinking her senna when Lady Tressilian's bell had rung. She had glanced at the clock and seen the time—twenty-five minutes past ten.

She had put on her dressing gown and come down.

She had heard a noise in the hall below and had looked over the balusters.

"It was Mr. Nevile just going out. He was taking his raincoat down from the hook."

"What suit was he wearing?"

"His grey pin stripe. His face was very worried and unhappy-looking. He shoved his arms into his coat as though he didn't care how he put it on. Then he went out and banged the front door behind him. I went on in to her ladyship. She was very drowsy, poor dear, and couldn't remember why she had rung for me—she couldn't always, poor lady. But I beat up her pillows and brought her a fresh glass of water and settled her comfortably."

"She didn't seem upset or afraid of anything?"

"Just tired, that's all. I was tired myself. Yawning. I went up and went right off to sleep."

That was Barrett's story and it seemed impossible to doubt her genuine grief and horror at the news of her mistress' death.

They went back to Lazenby's house and it was then that Battle announced that he had a question to ask.

"Ask away," said Lazenby.

"What time do you think Lady Tressilian died?"

"I've told you. Between ten o'clock and midnight."

"I know that's what you said. But it wasn't my question. I asked you what you, personally, *thought*?"

"Off the record, eh?"

"Yes."

"All right. My guess would be in the neighborhood of eleven o'clock."

"That's what I wanted you to say," said Battle.

"Glad to oblige. Why?"

"Never did like the idea of her being killed before 10:20. Take Barrett's sleeping draught—it wouldn't have got to work by then. That sleeping draught shows that the murder was meant to be committed a good deal later—during the night. I'd prefer midnight, myself."

"Could be. Eleven is only a guess."

"But it definitely couldn't be later than midnight?"

"No."

"It couldn't be after 2:30?"

"Good heavens, no."

"Well, that seems to let Strange out all right. I'll just have to check up on his movements after he left the house. If he's telling the truth, he's washed out and we can go on to our other suspects."

"The other people who inherit money?" suggested Leach.

"Maybe," said Battle. "But somehow, I don't think so. Someone with a kink, I'm looking for."

"A kink?"

"A nasty kink."


When they left the doctor's house they went down to the ferry. The ferry consisted of a rowing boat operated by two brothers, Will and George Barnes. The Barnes brothers knew everybody in Saltcreek by sight and most of the people who came over from Easterhead Bay. George said at once that Mr. Strange from Gull's Point had gone across at 10:30 on the preceding night. No, he had not brought Mr. Strange back again. Last ferry had gone at 1:30 from the Easterhead side and Mr. Strange wasn't on it.

Battle asked him if he knew Mr. Latimer.

"Latimer? Latimer? Tall, handsome young gentleman? Comes over from the hotel up to Gull's Point? Yes, I know him. Didn't see him at all last night, though. He's been over this morning. Went back last trip."

They crossed on the ferry and went up to the Easterhead Bay Hotel.

Here they found Mr. Latimer newly returned from the other side. He had crossed on the ferry before theirs.

Mr. Latimer was very anxious to do all he could to help.

"Yes, old Nevile came over last night. Looked very blue over something. Told me he'd had a row with the old lady. I hear he'd fallen out with Kay too, but he didn't tell me that, of course. Anyway, he was a bit down in the mouth. Seemed quite glad of my company for once in a way."

"He wasn't able to find you at once, I understand?" Latimer said sharply:

"Don't know why. I was sitting in the lounge. Strange said he looked in and didn't see me, but he wasn't in a state to concentrate. Or I may have strolled out into the gardens for five minutes or so. Always get out when I can. Beastly smell in this hotel. Noticed it last night in the bar. Drains, I think! Strange mentioned it too! We both smelt it. Nasty decayed smell. Might be a dead rat under the billiard room floor."

"You played billiards, and after your game?"

"Oh, we talked a bit, had another drink or two. Then Nevile said, 'Hullo, I've missed the ferry,' so I said I'd get out my car and drive him back, which I did. We got there about 2:30."

"And Mr. Strange was with you all the evening?"

"Oh, yes. Ask anybody. They'll tell you."

"Thank you, Mr. Latimer. We have to be so careful."

Leach said as they left the smiling, self-possessed young man:

"What's the idea of checking up so carefully on Nevile Strange?"

Battle smiled. Leach got it suddenly.

"Good Lord, it's the *other* one you're checking up on. So that's your idea."

"It's too soon to have ideas," said Battle. "I've just got to know exactly where Mr. Ted Latimer was last night. We know that from quarter past eleven say—to after midnight—he was with Nevile Strange. But where was he *before* that—when Strange arrived and couldn't find him?"

They pursued their inquiries doggedly—with bar attendants, waiters, lift boys. Latimer had been seen in the lounge room between nine and ten. He had been in the bar at a quarter past ten. But between that time and eleven twenty, he seemed to have been singularly elusive. Then one of the maids was found who declared that Mr. Latimer had been "in one of the small writing rooms with Mrs. Beddoes—that's the fat North country lady."

Pressed as to time she said she thought it was about eleven o'clock.

"That tears it," said Battle gloomily. "He was here all right. Just didn't want attention drawn to his fat (and no doubt rich) lady friend. That throws us back on those others—the servants, Kay Strange, Audrey Strange, Mary Aldin and Thomas Royde. *One* of them killed the old lady, but which? If we could find the real weapon—"

He stopped, then slapped his thigh.

"Got it, Jim, my boy! I know now what made me think of Hercule Poirot. We'll have a spot of lunch and go back to Gull's Point and I'll show you something."

## X

MARY ALDIN was restless. She went in and out of the house, picked off a dead dahlia head here and there, went back into the drawing room and shifted flower vases in an unmeaning fashion.

From the library came a vague murmur of voices. Mr. Trelawny was in there with Nevile. Kay and Audrey were nowhere to be seen.

Mary went out in the garden again. Down by the wall she spied Thomas Royde placidly smoking. She went and joined him.

"Oh, dear." She sat down beside him with a deep perplexed sigh.

"Anything the matter?" Thomas asked.

Mary laughed with a slight note of hysteria in the laugh.

"Nobody but you would say a thing like that. A murder in the house and you just say, 'Is anything the matter?'"

Looking a little surprised, Thomas said:

"I meant anything fresh?"

"Oh, I know what you meant. It's really a wonderful relief to find anyone so gloriously just-the-same-as-usual as you are!"

"Not much good, is it, getting all het up over things?"

"No, no. You're eminently sensible. It's how you manage to do it beats me."

"Well, I suppose I'm an outsider."

"That's true, of course. You can't feel the relief all the rest of us do that Nevile is cleared."

"I'm very pleased he is, of course," said Royde.

Mary shuddered.

"It was a very near thing. If Camilla hadn't taken it into her head to ring the bell for Barrett after Nevile had left her—"

She left the sentence unfinished. Thomas finished it for her.

"Then old Nevile would have been in for it all right."

He spoke with a certain grim satisfaction, then shook his head with a slight smile, as he met Mary's reproachful gaze.

"I'm not really heartless, but now that Nevile's all right I can't help being pleased he had a bit of a shaking up. He's always so damned complacent."

"He isn't really, Thomas."

"Perhaps not. It's just his manner. Anyway he was looking scared as hell this morning!"

"What a cruel streak you have!"

"Well, he's all right now. You know, Mary, even here Nevile has had the devil's own luck. Some other poor beggar with all that evidence piled up against him mightn't have had such a break."

Mary shivered again.

"Don't say that. I like to think the innocent are—protected."

"Do you, my dear?" His voice was gentle.

Mary burst out suddenly.

"Thomas, I'm worried. I'm frightfully worried."

"Yes."

"It's about Mr. Treves."

Thomas dropped his pipe on the stones. His voice changed as he bent to pick it up.

"What about Mr. Treves?"

"That night he was here—that story he told—about a little murderer! I've been wondering, Thomas. . . . Was it just a story? Or did he tell it with a purpose?"

"You mean," said Royde deliberately, "was it aimed at someone who was in the room?"

Mary whispered, "Yes."

Thomas said quietly:

"I've been trying to remember. . . . He told it, you know, what I was thinking about when you came along just now."

Mary half closed her eyes.

"I've been trying to remember. . . . He told it, you know, so very deliberately. . . . He almost dragged it into the conversation. And he said he would recognize the person anywhere. He emphasized that. As though he *had* recognized him."

"Mm," said Thomas. "I've been through all that."

"But why should he do it? What was the point?"

"I suppose," said Royde, "it was a kind of warning. Not to try anything on."

"You mean that Mr. Treves knew then that Camilla was going to be murdered?"

"N-o. I think that's too fantastic. It may have been just a general warning."

"What I've been wondering is, do you think we ought to tell the police?"

To that Thomas again gave his thoughtful consideration.

"I think not," he said at last. "I don't see that it's relevant in any way. It's not as though Treves were alive and could tell them anything."

"No," said Mary. "He's dead!" She gave a quick shiver. "It's so odd, Thomas, the way he died."

"Heart attack. He had a bad heart."

"I mean that curious business about the lift being out of order. *I don't like it.*"

"I don't like it very much myself," said Thomas Royde.

## XI

SUPERINTENDENT BATTLE looked round the bedroom. The bed had been made. Otherwise the room was unchanged. It had been neat when they first looked round it. It was neat now.

"That's it," said Superintendent Battle, pointing to the old-fashioned steel fender. "Do you see anything odd about that fender?"

"Must take some cleaning," said Jim Leach. "It's well kept. Nothing odd about it that I can see, except—yes, the left-hand knob is brighter than the right-hand one."

"That's what put Hercule Poirot into my head," said Battle. "You know his fad about things not being quite symmetrical—gets him all worked up. I suppose I thought unconsciously, 'That would worry old Poirot,' and then I began talking about him. Got your finger-print kit, Jones? We'll have a look at those two knobs."

Jones reported presently.

"There are prints on the right-hand knob, sir, none on the left."

"It's the left one we want, then. Those other prints are the housemaid's when she last cleaned it. That left-hand one has been cleaned since."

"There was a bit of screwed-up emery paper in this wastepaper basket," volunteered Jones. "I didn't think it meant anything."

"Because you didn't know what you were looking for, then. Gently now, I'll bet anything you like that knob unscrews—yes, I thought so."

Presently Jones held the knob up.

"It's a good weight," he said, weighing it in his hands.

Leach, bending over it, said:

"There's something dark—on the screw."

"Blood, as likely as not," said Battle. "Cleaned the knob itself and wiped it and that little stain on the screw wasn't noticed. I'll bet anything you like that's the weapon that caved the old lady's skull in. But there's more to find. It's up to you, Jones, to search the house again. This time you'll know exactly what you're looking for."

He gave a few swift detailed instructions. Going to the window, he put his head out.

"There's something yellow tucked into the ivy. That may be another piece of the puzzle. I rather think it is."

## XII

CROSSING THE HALL, Superintendent Battle was way-laid by Mary Aldin.

"Can I speak to you a minute, Superintendent?"

"Certainly, Miss Aldin. Shall we come in here?"

He threw open the dining-room door. Lunch had been cleared away by Hurstall.

"I want to ask you something, Superintendent. Surely you don't, you can't still think that this—that awful crime was done by one of us? It must have been some-one from outside! Some maniac!"

"You may not be far wrong there, Miss Aldin. Maniac is a word that describes this criminal very well if I'm not mistaken. But not an outsider."

Her eyes opened very wide.

"Do you mean that someone in this house is—is *mad?*"

"You're thinking," said the Superintendent, "of someone foaming at the mouth and rolling their eyes. Mania isn't like that. Some of the most dangerous crim-inal lunatics have looked as sane as you or I. It's a question, usually, of having an obsession. One idea, preying on the mind, gradually distorting it. Pathetic, reasonable people who come up to you and explain how they're being persecuted and how everyone is spy-ing on them—and you sometimes feel it must all be true."

"I'm sure nobody here has any ideas of being perse-cuted."

"I only gave that as an instance. There are other forms of insanity. But I believe whoever committed this crime was under the domination of one fixed idea—an idea on which they had brooded until—literally—noth-ing else mattered or had any importance."

Mary shivered. She said:

"There's something, I think, you ought to know."

Concisely and clearly she told him of Mr. Treves'
visit to dinner and of the story he had told. Superintendent Battle was deeply interested. "He said he could
recognize this person?—man or woman, by the way?"

"I took it that it was a boy the story was about—but
it's true Mr. Treves didn't actually say so—in fact I remember now—he distinctly stated he would not give
any particulars as to sex or age."

"Did he? Rather significant, perhaps. And he said
there was a definite physical peculiarity by which he
could be sure of knowing this child anywhere."

"Yes."

"A scar, perhaps—has anybody here got a scar?"

He noticed the faint hesitation before Mary Aldin
replied:

"Not that I have noticed."

"Come now, Miss Aldin." He smiled. "You *have*
noticed something. If so, don't you think that I shall be
able to notice it, too?"

She shook her head.

"I—I haven't noticed anything of the kind."

But he saw that she was startled and upset. His words
had obviously suggested a very unpleasant train of
thought to her. He wished he knew just what it was, but
his experience made him aware that to press her at this
minute would not yield any result.

He brought the conversation back to old Mr. Treves.

Mary told him of the tragic sequel to the evening.

Battle questioned her at some length. Then he said
quietly:

"That's a new one on me. Never come across that
before."

"What do you mean?"

"I've never come across a murder committed by the simple expedient of hanging a placard on a lift."

She looked horrified.

"You don't really think—"

"That it was murder? Of course it was! Quick, resourceful murder. It might not have come off, of course —but it *did* come off."

"Just because Mr. Treves knew—"

"Yes. Because he would have been able to direct our attention to one particular person in this house. As it is, we've started in the dark. But we've got a glimmer of light now, and every minute the case is getting clearer. I'll tell you this, Miss Aldin—this murder was very carefully planned beforehand down to the smallest detail. And I want to impress one thing on your mind —don't let anybody know that you've told me what you have. That is important. Don't tell *anyone*, mind."

Mary nodded. She was still looking dazed.

Superintendent Battle went out of the room and proceeded to do what he had been about to do when Mary Aldin intercepted him. He was a methodical man. He wanted certain information, and a new and promising hare did not distract him from the orderly performance of his duties, however tempting this new hare might be.

He tapped on the library door, and Nevile Strange's voice called, "Come in."

Battle was introduced to Mr. Trelawny, a tall, distinguished-looking man with a keen dark eye.

"Sorry if I am butting in," said Superintendent Battle apologetically. "But there's something I haven't got clear. You, Mr. Strange, inherit half the late Sir Matthew's estate, but who inherits the other half?"

Nevile looked surprised.

"I told you. My wife."

"Yes. But—" Battle coughed in a deprecating manner, "which wife, Mr. Strange?"

"Oh, I see. Yes, I expressed myself badly. The money goes to Audrey who was my wife at the time the will was made. That's right, Mr. Trelawny?"

The lawyer assented.

"The bequest is quite clearly worded. The estate is to be divided between Sir Matthew's ward Nevile Henry Strange, and his wife Audrey Elizabeth Strange née Standish. The subsequent divorce makes no difference whatever."

"That's clear, then," said Battle. "I take it Mrs. Audrey Strange is fully aware of these facts?"

"Certainly," said Mr. Trelawny.

"And the present Mrs. Strange?"

"Kay?" Nevile looked slightly surprised. "Oh, I suppose so. At least—I've never talked much about it with her—"

"I think you'll find," said Battle, "that's she's under a misapprehension. She thinks that the money on Lady Tressilian's death comes to you and your *present* wife. At least, that's what she gave me to understand this morning. That's why I came along to find out how the position really lay."

"How extraordinary," said Nevile. "Still, I suppose it might have happened quite easily. She said once or twice now that I think about it, 'We come into that money when Camilla dies,' but I suppose I assumed that she was just associating herself with me in my share of it."

"It's extraordinary," said Battle, "the amount of misunderstandings there are even between two people who discuss a thing quite often—both of them assuming different things and neither of them discovering the discrepancy."

"I suppose so," said Nevile, not sounding very interested. "It doesn't matter much in this case, anyway. It's

not as though we're short of money at all. I'm very glad
for Audrey. She has been very hard up and this will
make a big difference to her."

Battle said bluntly:

"But, surely, sir, at the time of the divorce, she was
entitled to an allowance from you?"

Nevile flushed. He said in a constrained voice:

"There is such a thing as—as pride, Superintendent.
Audrey has always persistently refused to touch a penny
of the allowance I wished to make her."

"A very generous allowance," put in Mr. Trelawny.
"But Mrs. Audrey Strange has always returned it and
refused to accept it."

"Very interesting," said Battle and went out before
anyone could ask him to elaborate that comment.

He went and found his nephew.

"On its face value," he said, "there's a nice monetary
motive for nearly everybody in this case. Nevile Strange
and Audrey Strange get a cool fifty thousand each. Kay
Strange thinks she's entitled to fifty thousand. Mary
Aldin gets an income that frees her from having to earn
her living. Thomas Royde, I'm bound to say, doesn't
gain. But we can include Hurstall and even Barrett if
we admit that she'd take the risk of finishing herself off
to avoid suspicion. Yes, as I say, there are no lack of
money motives. And yet, if I'm right, money doesn't
enter into this at all. If there's such a thing as a murder
for pure hate, this is it. And if no one comes along and
throws a spanner into the works, I'm going to get the
person who did it!"

Afterwards he wondered what had put that particular
phrase into his head just then—Andrew MacWhirter
had been around at Easterhead Bay on the preceding
Saturday.

## XIII

ANDREW MACWHIRTER sat on the terrace of the
Easterhead Bay Hotel and stared across the river to the
frowning height of Stark Head opposite.

He was engaged at the moment in a careful stocktak-
ing of his thoughts and emotions.

Here, seven months ago, he had attempted to take his
own life. Chance, nothing but chance, had intervened.
Was he, he wondered, grateful to that chance?

He decided, soberly, that he was not. True, he felt
no present disposition to take his life. That phase was
over for good. He was willing to address himself now
to the task of living, not with enthusiasm nor even with
pleasure, but in a methodical day-after-day spirit. You
could not, that he admitted, take your own life in cold
blood. There had to be some extra fillip of despair, of
grief, of desperation or of passion. You could not commit suicide merely because you felt that life was a
dreary round of uninteresting happenings.

He was now, he supposed, to be considered quite a
fortunate man. Fate, after having frowned, had smiled
instead. But he was in no mood to smile back. His sense
of humor was grimly tickled when he thought of the
interview to which he had been summoned by that rich
and eccentric peer Lord Cornelly.

"You're MacWhirter? You were with Herbert Clay?
Clay got his driving license endorsed, all because you
wouldn't say he was going at twenty miles an hour.
Livid he was! Told us about it one night at the Savoy.
'Damned pig-headed Scot!' he said. I thought to myself
—that's the kind of chap *I* want! Man who can't be
bribed to tell lies. You won't have to tell lies for me. I
don't do my business that way. I go about the world

looking for honest men—and there are damned few of them."

The little peer had cackled with laughter, his shrewd monkey-like face wrinkled up with mirth. MacWhirter had stood stolidly, not amused.

But he had got the job. A good job. His future now was assured. In a week's time he was to leave England for South America.

He hardly knew what it was that had made him choose to spend his few last days of leisure where he now was. Yet something had drawn him there. Perhaps the wish to test himself—to see if there remained in his heart any of the old despair.

Mona? How little he cared now. She was married to the other man. He had passed her in the street one day without feeling any emotion. He could remember his grief and bitterness when she left him, but they were past now and gone.

He was recalled from these thoughts by an impact of wet dog and the frenzied appeal of a newly made friend, Miss Diana Brinton, aged thirteen.

"Oh, come away, Don. Come *away*. Isn't it awful? He's rolled on some fish or something down on the beach. You can smell him yards away. The fish was awfully dead, you know."

MacWhirter's nose confirmed this assumption.

"In a sort of crevice on the rocks," said Miss Brinton. "I took him into the sea and tried to wash it off, but it doesn't seem to have done much good."

MacWhirter agreed. Don, a wire-haired terrier of amiable and loving disposition, was looking hurt by the tendency of his friends to keep him firmly at arm's length.

"Sea water's no good," said MacWhirter. "Hot water and soap's the only thing."

"I know. But that's not so jolly easy in a hotel. We haven't got a private bath."

In the end MacWhirter and Diana surreptitiously entered by the side door with Don on a lead, and smuggling him up to MacWhirter's bathroom, a thorough cleansing took place and both MacWhirter and Diana got very wet. Don was very sad when it was all over. That disgusting smell of soap again—just when he had found a really nice perfume such as any other dog would envy. Oh, well, it was always the same with humans—they had no decent sense of smell.

The little incident had left MacWhirter in a more cheerful mood. He took the bus into Saltington, where he had left a suit to be cleaned.

The girl in charge of the 24-Hour Cleaners looked at him vacantly.

"MacWhirter, did you say? I'm afraid it isn't ready yet."

"It should be." He had been promised that suit the day before and even that would have been 48 and not 24 hours. A woman might have said all this. MacWhirter merely scowled.

"There's not been time yet," said the girl, smiling indifferently.

"Nonsense."

The girl stopped smiling. She snapped.

"Anyway it's not done," she said.

"Then I'll take it away as it is," said MacWhirter.

"Nothing's been done to it," the girl warned him.

"I'll take it away."

"I daresay we might get it done by tomorrow—as a special favor."

"I'm not in the habit of asking for special favors. Just give me the suit, please."

Giving him a bad-tempered look, the girl went into a

back room. She returned with a clumsily done up parcel which she pushed across the counter.

MacWhirter took it and went out.

He felt, quite ridiculously, as though he had won a victory. Actually it merely meant that he would have to have the suit cleaned elsewhere!

He threw the parcel on his bed when he returned to the hotel and looked at it with annoyance. Perhaps he could get it sponged and pressed in the hotel. It was not really too bad—perhaps it didn't actually need cleaning?

He undid the parcel and gave vent to an expression of annoyance. Really, the 24-Hour Cleaners were too inefficient for words. This wasn't his suit. It wasn't even the same color! It had been a dark blue suit he had left with them. Impertinent, inefficient muddlers.

He glanced irritably at the label. It had the name MacWhirter all right. Another MacWhirter? Or some stupid interchange of labels.

Staring down vexedly at the crumpled heap, he suddenly sniffed.

Surely he knew that smell—particularly unpleasant smell . . . connected somehow with a dog. Yes, that was it. Diana and her dog. Absolutely and literally stinking fish!

He bent down and examined the suit. There it was, a discolored patch on the shoulder of the coat. On the *shoulder*—

Now that, thought MacWhirter, is really very curious. . . .

Anyway, next day, he would have a few grim words with the girl at the 24-Hour Cleaners. Gross mismanagement!

## XIV

AFTER DINNER, he strolled out of the hotel and down the road to the ferry. It was a clear night, but cold, with a sharp foretaste of winter. Summer was over.

MacWhirter crossed in the ferry to the Saltcreek side. It was the second time that he was revisiting Stark Head. The place had a fascination for him. He walked slowly up the hill, passing the Balmoral Court Hotel and then a big house set on the point of a cliff. Gull's Point— he read the name on the painted door. Of course, that was where the old lady had been murdered. There had been a lot of talk in the hotel about it, his chambermaid had insisted on telling him all about it and the newspapers had given it a prominence which had annoyed Mac-Whirter, who preferred to read of world-wide affairs and who was not interested in crime.

He went on, down hill again to skirt a small beach and some old-fashioned fishing cottages that had been modernized. Then up again till the road ended and petered out into the track that led up on Stark Head.

It was grim and forbidding on Stark Head. Mac-Whirter stood on the cliff edge looking down to the sea. So he had stood on that other night. He tried to recapture some of the feeling he had then—the desperation, anger, weariness—the longing to be out of it all. But there was nothing to recapture. All that had gone. There was instead a cold anger. Caught on that tree, rescued by coast guards, fussed over like a naughty child in hospital, a series of indignities and affronts. Why couldn't he have been *let alone?* He would rather, a thousand times rather, be out of it all. He still felt that. The only thing he had lost was the necessary impetus.

How it had hurt him then to think of Mona! He could think of her quite calmly now. She had always

been rather a fool. Easily taken by anyone who flattered
her or played up to her idea of herself. Very pretty. Yes,
very pretty—but no mind. Not the kind of woman he
had once dreamed about.

But that was beauty, of course— Some vague fancied
picture of a woman flying through the night with white
draperies flying out behind her . . . Something like the
figurehead of a ship—only not so bold . . . not nearly
so solid . . .

And then, with dramatic suddenness, the incredible
happened! Out of the night came a flying figure. One
minute she was not there, the next minute she was—a
white figure running—running— to the cliff's edge. A
figure, beautiful and desperate, driven to destruction by
pursuing Furies! Running with a terrible desperation. . . . He knew that desperation. He knew what it
meant. . . .

He came with a rush out of the shadows and caught
her just as she was about to go over the edge!

He said fiercely:

"No, you don't. . . ."

It was just like holding a bird. She struggled—struggled silently, and then, again like a bird, was suddenly
dead still.

He said urgently:

"Don't throw yourself over! Nothing's worth it. *Nothing!* Even if you are desperately unhappy—"

She made a sound. It was, perhaps, a far-off ghost of
a laugh.

He said sharply:

"You're not unhappy? What is it then?"

She answered him at once with the low softly-
breathed word:

*"Afraid."*

"Afraid?" He was so astonished he let her go, standing back a pace to see her better.

He realized then the truth of her words. It was fear that had lent that urgency to her footsteps. It was fear that made her small white intelligent face blank and stupid. Fear that dilated those wide-apart eyes.

He said incredulously:

"What are you afraid of?"

She replied so low that he hardly heard it.

*"I'm afraid of being hanged. . . ."*

Yes, she had said just that. He stared and stared. He looked from her to the cliff edge.

"So that's why?"

"Yes. A quick death instead of—" She closed her eyes and shivered. She went on shivering.

MacWhirter was piecing things together logically in his mind.

He said at last:

"Lady Tressilian? The old lady who was murdered." Then, accusingly: "You'll be Mrs. Strange—the first Mrs. Strange."

Still shivering, she nodded her head.

MacWhirter went on in his slow careful voice, trying to remember all that he had heard. Rumor had been incorporated with fact.

"They detained your husband—that's right, isn't it? A lot of evidence against him—and then they found that that evidence had been faked by someone. . . ."

He stopped and looked at her. She wasn't shivering any longer. She was just standing looking at him like a docile child. He found her attitude unendurably affecting.

His voice went on:

"I see. . . . Yes, I see how it was. . . . He left you for another woman, didn't he? And you loved him. . . . That's why—" He broke off. He said, "I understand. My wife left me for another man. . . ."

She flung out her arms. She began stammering wildly, hopelessly:

"It's n-n-not—it's n-n-not l-like that. N-not at all—"
He cut her short. His voice was stern and commanding.

"Go home! *You needn't be afraid any longer.* D'you hear? *I'll* see that you're not hanged!"

### XV

MARY ALDIN was lying on the drawing-room sofa. Her head ached and her whole body felt worn out.

The inquest had taken place the day before, and after formal evidence of identification, had been adjourned for a week.

Lady Tressilian's funeral was to take place on the morrow. Audrey and Kay had gone into Saltington in the car to get some black clothes. Ted Latimer had gone with them. Nevile and Thomas Royde had gone for a walk, so except for the servants, Mary was alone in the house.

Superintendent Battle and Inspector Leach had been absent today, and that, too, was a relief. It seemed to Mary that with their absence a shadow had lifted. They had been polite, quite pleasant, in fact, but the ceaseless questions, that quiet deliberate probing and sifting of every fact was the sort of thing that wore hardly on the nerves. By now that wooden-faced Superintendent must have learned of every incident, every word, every gesture, even, of the past ten days.

Now, with their going, there was peace. Mary let herself relax. She would forget everything—everything. Just lie back and rest.

"Excuse me, Madam—"

It was Hurstall in the doorway, looking apologetic.

"Yes, Hurstall?"

"A gentleman wishes to see you. I have put him in the study."

Mary looked at him in astonishment and some annoyance.

"Who is it?"

"He gave his name as Mr. MacWhirter, Miss."

"I've never heard of him."

"No, Miss."

"He must be a reporter. You shouldn't have let him in, Hurstall."

Hurstall coughed.

"I don't think he is a reporter, Miss. I think he is a friend of Miss Audrey's."

"Oh, that's different."

Smoothing her hair, Mary went wearily across the hall and into the small study. She was, somehow, a little surprised as the tall man standing by the window turned. He did not look in the least like a friend of Audrey's.

However she said pleasantly:

"I'm sorry Mrs. Strange is out. You wanted to see her?"

He looked at her in a thoughtful considering way.

"You'll be Miss Aldin?" he said.

"Yes."

"I daresay you can help me just as well. I want to find some rope."

"Rope?" said Mary in lively amazement.

"Yes, rope. Where would you be likely to keep a piece of rope?"

Afterwards Mary considered that she had been half-hypnotized. If this strange man had volunteered any explanation she might have resisted. But Andrew Mac-Whirter, unable to think of a plausible explanation, decided, very wisely, to do without one. He just stated quite simply what he wanted. She found herself, semi-dazed, leading MacWhirter in search of rope.

"What kind of rope?" she had asked.

And he had replied:

"Any rope will do."

She said doubtfully:

"Perhaps in the potting shed——"

"Shall we go there?"

She led the way. There was twine and an odd bit of cord, but MacWhirter shook his head.

He wanted rope—a good-sized coil of rope.

"There's the box room," said Mary hesitatingly.

"Ay, that might be the place."

They went indoors and upstairs. Mary threw open the box-room door. MacWhirter stood in the doorway looking in. He gave a curious sigh of contentment.

"There it is," he said.

There was a big coil of rope lying on a chest just inside the door in company with old fishing tackle and some moth-eaten cushions. He laid a hand on her arm and impelled Mary gently forward until they stood looking down on the rope. He touched it and said:

"I'd like you to charge your memory with this, Miss Aldin. You'll notice that everything round about is covered with dust. *There's no dust on this rope.* Just feel it."

She said:

"It feels slightly damp," in a surprised tone.

"Just so."

He turned to go out again.

"But the rope? I thought you wanted it?" said Mary in surprise.

MacWhirter smiled.

"I just wanted to know it was there. That's all. Perhaps you wouldn't mind locking this door, Miss Aldin —and taking the key out? Yes. I'd be obliged if you'd hand the key to Superintendent Battle or Inspector Leach. It would be best in their keeping."

As they went downstairs, Mary made an effort to rally herself.

She protested as they reached the main hall:

"But really, I don't understand—"

"There's no need for you to understand." He took her hand and shook it heartily. "I'm very much obliged to you for your co-operation."

Whereupon he went straight out of the front door.

Nevile and Thomas came in presently and the car arrived back shortly afterwards and Mary Aldin found herself envying Kay and Ted for being able to look quite cheerful. They were laughing and joking together. After all, why not? she thought. Camilla Tressilian had been nothing to Kay. All this tragic business was very hard on a bright young creature.

They had just finished lunch when the police came. There was something scared in Hurstall's voice as he announced that Superintendent Battle and Inspector Leach were in the drawing room.

Superintendent Battle's face was quite genial as he greeted them.

"Hope I haven't disturbed you all," he said apologetically. "But there are one or two things I'd like to know about. This glove, for instance, who does it belong to?"

He held it out, a small yellow chamois leather glove. He addressed Audrey.

"Is it yours, Mrs. Strange?"

She shook her head.

"No—no, it isn't mine."

"Miss Aldin?"

"I don't think so. I have none of that color."

"May I see?" Kay held out her hand. "No."

"Perhaps you'd just slip it on."

Kay tried, but the glove was too small.

"Miss Aldin?"

Mary tried in her turn.

"It's too small for you also," said Battle. He turned back to Audrey. "I think you'll find it fits you all right. Your hand is smaller than either of the other ladies."

Audrey took it from him and slipped it on over her right hand.

Nevile Strange said sharply:

"She's already told you, Battle, that it isn't her glove."

"Ah, well," said Battle, "perhaps she made a mistake. Or forgot."

Audrey said: "It may be mine—gloves are so alike, aren't they?"

Battle said:

"At any rate it was found outside your window, Mrs. Strange, pushed down into the ivy—*with its fellow.*"

There was a pause. Audrey opened her mouth to speak, then closed it up again. Her eyes fell before the Superintendent's steady gaze.

Nevile sprang forward.

"Look here, Superintendent—"

"Perhaps we might have a word with you, Mr. Strange, privately?" Battle said gravely.

"Certainly, Superintendent. Come into the library."

He led the way and the two police officers followed him.

As soon as the door had closed Nevile said sharply:

"What's this ridiculous story about gloves outside my wife's window?"

Battle said quietly:

"Mr. Strange, we've found some very curious things in this house."

Nevile frowned.

"Curious? What do you mean by curious?"

"I'll show you."

In obedience to a nod, Leach left the room and came back holding a very strange implement.

Battle said:

"This consists, as you see, sir, of a steel ball taken from a Victorian fender—a heavy steel ball. Then the head has been sawed off a tennis racket and the ball has been screwed into the handle of the racket." He paused. "I think there can be no doubt that this is what was used to kill Lady Tressilian."

"Horrible!" said Nevile with a shudder. "But where did you find this—this nightmare?"

"The ball had been cleaned and put back on the fender. The murderer had, however, neglected to clean the screw. We found a trace of blood on that. In the same way the handle and the head of the racket were joined together again by means of adhesive surgical plaster. It was then thrown carelessly back into the cupboard under the stairs where it would probably have remained quite unnoticed amongst so many others if we hadn't happened to be looking for something of that kind."

"Smart of you, Superintendent."

"Just a matter of routine."

"No fingerprints, I suppose?"

"That racket which belongs by its weight, I should say, to Mrs. Kay Strange, has been handled by her and also by you and both your prints are on it. *But it also shows unmistakable signs that someone wearing gloves handled it after you two did.* There was just one other fingerprint—left this time in inadvertence, I think. That was on the surgical strapping that had been applied to bind the racket together again. I'm not going for the moment to say whose print that was. I've got some other points to mention first."

Battle paused, then he said:

"I want you to prepare yourself for a shock, Mr.

Strange. And first I want to ask you something. Are you quite sure that it was your own idea to have this meeting here and that it was not actually suggested to you by Mrs. Audrey Strange?"

"Audrey did nothing of the sort. Audrey——"

The door opened and Thomas Royde came in.

"Sorry to butt in," he said, "but I thought I'd like to be in on this."

Nevile turned a harassed face towards him.

"Do you mind, old fellow? This is all rather private."

"I'm afraid I don't care about that. You see, I heard a name outside." He paused. "Audrey's name."

"And what the hell has Audrey's name got to do with you?" demanded Nevile, his temper rising.

"Well, what has it to do with you if it comes to that? I haven't said anything definite to Audrey, but I came here meaning to ask her to marry me, and I think she knows it. What's more, I mean to marry her."

Superintendent Battle coughed. Nevile turned to him with a start.

"Sorry, Superintendent. This interruption——"

Battle said:

"It doesn't matter to me, Mr. Strange. I've got one more question to ask you. That dark blue coat you wore at dinner the night of the murder, it's got fair hairs inside the collar and on the shoulders. Do you know how they got there?"

"I suppose they're my hairs."

"Oh, no, they're not yours, sir. They're a lady's hairs, and there's a red hair on the sleeves."

"I suppose that's my wife's—Kay's. The others, you are suggesting, are Audrey's? Very likely they are. I caught my cuff button in her hair one night outside on the terrace, I remember."

"In that case," murmured Inspector Leach, "the fair hair would be on the cuff."

"What the devil are you suggesting?" cried Nevile.

"There's a trace of powder, too, inside the coat collar," said Battle. "Primavera Naturelle No. 1—a very pleasant-scented powder and expensive—but it's no good telling me that you use it, Mr. Strange, because I shan't believe you. And Mrs. Kay Strange uses Orchid Sun Kiss. Mrs. Audrey Strange does use Primavera Naturelle 1."

"What are you suggesting?" repeated Nevile.

Battle leaned forward.

"I'm suggesting that—on some occasion *Mrs. Audrey Strange wore that coat.* It's the only reasonable way the hair and the powder could get where they did. Then you've seen that glove I produced just now? It's her glove all right. That was the right hand, *here's the left*—" He drew it out of his pocket and put it down on the table. It was crumpled and stained with rusty brown patches.

Nevile said with a note of fear in his voice: "What's that on it?"

"Blood, Mr. Strange," said Battle firmly. "And you'll note this, it's the *left* hand. Now Mrs. Audrey Strange is left-handed. I noted that first thing when I saw her sitting with her coffee cup in her right hand and her cigarette in her left at the breakfast table. And the pen tray on her writing-table had been shifted to the left-hand side. It all fits in. The knob from her grate, the gloves outside her window, the hair and powder on the coat. Lady Tressilian was struck on the right temple—but the position of the bed made it impossible for anyone to have stood on the other side of it. It follows that to strike Lady Tressilian a blow with the right hand would be a very awkward thing to do—but it's the natural way to strike for a *left-handed* person. . . ."

Nevile laughed scornfully.

"Are you suggesting that Audrey—*Audrey* would

make all these elaborate preparations and strike down an old lady whom she had known for years in order to get her hands on that old lady's money?"

Battle shook his head.

"I'm suggesting nothing of the sort. I'm sorry, Mr. Strange, you've got to understand just how things are. This crime, first, last and all the time was directed against *you*. Ever since you left her, Audrey Strange has been brooding over the possibilities of revenge. In the end she has become mentally unbalanced. Perhaps she was never mentally very strong. She thought, perhaps, of killing you but that wasn't enough. She thought at last of getting you hanged for murder. She chose an evening when she knew you had quarreled with Lady Tressilian. She took the coat from your bedroom and wore it when she struck the old lady down so that it should be blood-stained. She put your niblick on the floor knowing we would find your fingerprints on it and smeared blood and hair on the head of the club. It was she who instilled into your mind the idea of coming here when she was here. And the thing that saved you was the one thing she couldn't count on—the fact that Lady Tressilian rang her bell for Barrett and that Barrett saw you leave the house."

Nevile had buried his face in his hands. He said now:

"It's not true. It's not true! Audrey's never borne a grudge against me. You've got the whole thing wrong. She's the straightest, truest creature—without one thought of evil in her heart."

Battle sighed.

"It's not my business to argue with you, Mr. Strange. I only wanted to prepare you. I shall caution Mrs. Strange and ask her to accompany me. I've got the warrant. You'd better see about getting a solicitor for her."

"It's preposterous. Absolutely preposterous."

"Love turns to hate more easily than you think, Mr. Strange."

"I tell you it's all wrong—preposterous."

Thomas Royde broke in. His voice was quiet and pleasant.

"Do stop repeating that it's preposterous, Nevile. Pull yourself together. Don't you see that the only thing that can help Audrey now is for you to give up all your ideas of chivalry and come out with the truth?"

"The truth? You mean—"

"I mean the truth about Audrey and Adrian." Royde turned to the police officers. "You see, Superintendent, you've got the facts wrong. Nevile didn't leave Audrey. She left him. She ran away with my brother Adrian. Then Adrian was killed in a car accident. Nevile behaved with the utmost chivalry to Audrey. He arranged that she should divorce him and that he would take the blame."

"Didn't want her name dragged through the mud," muttered Nevile sulkily. "Didn't know anyone knew."

"Adrian wrote out to me, just before," explained Thomas briefly. He went on: "Don't you see, Superintendent, that knocks your motive out! Audrey has no cause to hate Nevile. On the contrary, she has every reason to be grateful to him. He's tried to get her to accept an allowance which she wouldn't do. Naturally when he wanted her to come and meet Kay she didn't feel she could refuse."

"You see," Nevile put in eagerly. "That cuts out her motive. Thomas is right."

Battle's wooden face was immovable.

"Motive's only one thing," he said. "I may have been wrong about that. But facts are another. All the facts show that she's guilty."

Nevile said meaningly:

"All the facts showed that *I* was guilty two days ago!"

Battle seemed a little taken aback.

"That's true enough. But look here, Mr. Strange, at what you're asking me to believe. You're asking me to believe that there's someone who hates both of you—someone who, if the plot against you failed, had laid a second trail to lead to Audrey Strange. Now can you think of anyone, Mr. Strange, who hates both you *and* your former wife?"

Nevile's head had dropped into his hands again.

"When you say it like that, you make it all sound fantastic!"

"Because it *is* fantastic. I've got to go by the facts. If Mrs. Strange has any explanation to offer—"

"Did I have any explanation?" asked Nevile.

"It's no good, Mr. Strange. I've got to do my duty."

Battle got up abruptly. He and Leach left the room first. Nevile and Royde came close behind them.

They went on across the hall into the drawing room. There they stopped.

Audrey Strange got up. She walked forward to meet them. She looked straight at Battle, her lips parted in what was very nearly a smile.

She said very softly:

"You want me, don't you?"

Battle became very official.

"Mrs. Strange, I have a warrant here for your arrest on the charge of murdering Camilla Tressilian on Monday last, September twelfth. I must caution you that anything you say will be written down and may be used in evidence at your trial."

Audrey gave a sigh. Her small clear-cut face was peaceful and pure as a cameo.

"It's almost a relief. I'm glad it's—over!"

Nevile sprang forward.

"Audrey—don't say anything—don't speak at all."

She smiled at him.

"But why not, Nevile? It's all true—and I'm so tired."

Leach drew a deep breath. Well, that was that. Mad as a hatter, of course, but it would save a lot of worry! He wondered what had happened to his uncle. The old boy was looking as though he had seen a ghost. Staring at the demented creature as though he couldn't believe his eyes. Oh, well, it had been an interesting case, Leach thought comfortably.

And then, an almost grotesque anticlimax, Hurstall opened the drawing room door and announced:

"Mr. MacWhirter."

MacWhirter strode in purposefully. He went straight up to Battle.

"Are you the police officer in charge of the Tressilian case?" he asked.

"I am."

"Then I have an important statement to make. I am sorry not to have come forward before, but the importance of something I happened to see on the night of Monday last has only just dawned on me." He gave a quick glance round the room. "If I can speak to you somewhere?"

Battle turned to Leach.

"Will you stay here with Mrs. Strange?"

Leach said officially:

"Yes, sir."

Then he leaned forward and whispered something into the other's ear.

Battle turned to MacWhirter.

"Come this way."

He led the way into the library.

"Now, then, what's all this? My colleague tells me that he's seen you before—last winter?"

"Quite right," said MacWhirter. "Attempted suicide. That's part of my story."

"Go on, Mr. MacWhirter."

"Last January I attempted to kill myself by throwing myself off Stark Head. This year, the fancy took me to revisit the spot. I walked up there on Monday night. I stood there for some time. I looked down at the sea and across to Easterhead Bay and I then looked to my left. That is to say I looked across towards this house. I could see it quite plainly in the moonlight."

"Yes."

"Until today I had not realized *that that was the night when a murder was committed.*"

He leant forward.

"I'll tell you what I saw."

## XVI

IT WAS REALLY only about five minutes before Battle returned to the drawing room, but to those there it seemed much longer.

Kay had suddenly lost control of herself. She had cried out to Audrey:

"I knew it was you. I always knew it was you. I knew you were up to something—"

Mary Aldin said quickly:

"Please, Kay."

Nevile said sharply:

"Shut up, Kay, for God's sake."

Ted Latimer came over to Kay, who had begun to cry.

"Get a grip on yourself," he said kindly.

He said to Nevile angrily:

"You don't seem to realize that Kay has been under a lot of strain! Why don't you look after her a bit, Strange?"

"I'm all right," said Kay.

"For two pins," said Ted, "I'd take you away from the lot of them!"

Inspector Leach cleared his throat. A lot of injudicious things were said at times like these, as he well knew. The unfortunate part was that they were usually remembered most inconveniently afterwards.

Battle came back into the room. His face was expressionless.

He said: "Will you put one or two things together, Mrs. Strange? I'm afraid Inspector Leach must come upstairs with you."

Mary Aldin said:

"I'll come too."

When the two women had left the room with the Inspector, Nevile said anxiously:

"Well, what did that chap want?"

Battle said slowly:

"Mr. MacWhirter tells a very odd story."

"Does it help Audrey? Are you still determined to arrest her?"

"I've told you, Mr. Strange. I've got to do my duty."

Nevile turned away, the eagerness dying out of his face.

He said:

"I'd better telephone Trelawny, I suppose."

"There's no immediate hurry for that, Mr. Strange. There's a certain experiment I want to make first as a result of Mr. MacWhirter's statement. I'll just see that Mrs. Strange gets off first."

Audrey was coming down the stairs, Inspector Leach beside her. Her face still had that remote, detached composure.

Nevile came towards her, his hands outstretched.

"Audrey—"

Her colorless glance swept over him. She said:

"It's all right, Nevile. I don't mind. I don't mind anything."

Thomas Royde stood by the front door, almost as though he would bar the way out.

A very faint smile came to her lips.

" 'True Thomas,' " she murmured.

He mumbled:

"If there's anything I can do—"

"No one can do anything," said Audrey.

She went out with her head high. A police car was waiting outside with Sergeant Jones in it. Audrey and Leach got in.

Ted Latimer murmured appreciatively:

"Lovely exit!"

Nevile turned on him furiously. Superintendent Battle dexterously interposed his bulk and raised a soothing voice:

"As I said, I've got an experiment to make. Mr. Mac-Whirter is waiting down at the ferry. We're to join him there in ten minutes' time. We shall be going out in a motor lunch, so the ladies had better wrap up warmly. In ten minutes, please."

He might have been a stage manager, ordering a company on to the stage. He took no notice at all of their puzzled faces.

# ZERO HOUR

## I

IT WAS CHILLY on the water and Kay hugged the little fur jacket she was wearing closer round her.

The launch chugged down the river below Gull's Point, and then swung round into the little bay that divided Gull's Point from the frowning mass of Stark Head.

Once or twice, a question began to be asked, but each time Superintendent Battle held up a large hand rather like a cardboard ham, intimating that the time had not come yet. So the silence was unbroken save for the rushing of the water past them. Kay and Ted stood together looking down into the water. Nevile was slumped down, his legs stuck out. Mary Aldin and Thomas Royde sat up in the bow. And one and all glanced from time to time curiously at the tall aloof figure of MacWhirter by the stern. He looked at none of them, but stood with his back turned and his shoulders hunched up.

Not until they were under the frowning shadow of Stark Head, did Battle throttle down the engine and begin to speak his piece.

He spoke without self-consciousness and in a tone that was more reflective than anything else.

"This has been a very odd case—one of the oddest I've ever known, and I'd like to say something on the subject of murder generally. What I'm going to say is not original—actually I overheard young Mr. Daniels, the K.C., say something of the kind, and I wouldn't be surprised if *he'd* got it from someone else—he's a trick of doing that!

"It's this! When you read the account of a murder—or say, a fiction story based on murder, you usually begin with the murder itself. That's all wrong. The murder begins a *long time beforehand*. A murder is the culmination of a lot of different circumstances, all converging at a given moment at a given point. People are brought into it from different parts of the globe and for unforeseen reasons. Mr. Royde is here from Malaya. Mr. MacWhirter is here because he wanted to revisit a spot where he once tried to commit suicide. The murder itself is the *end* of the story. It's Zero Hour."

He paused.

*"It's Zero Hour now."*

Five faces were turned to him—only five, for MacWhirter did not turn his head. Five puzzled faces.

Mary Aldin said:

"You mean that Lady Tressilian's death was the culmination of a long train of circumstances?"

"No, Miss Aldin, not Lady Tressilian's death. Lady Tressilian's death was only incidental to the main object of the murderer. The murder I am talking of *is the murder of Audrey Strange.*"

He listened to the sharp indrawing of breath. He wondered if, suddenly, someone was afraid. . . .

"This crime was planned quite a long time ago—probably as early as last winter. It was planned down to the smallest detail. It had one object, and one object only: that Audrey Strange should be hanged by the neck till she was dead. . . .

"It was very cunningly planned by someone who thought himself very clever. Murderers are usually vain. There was first the superficial unsatisfactory evidence against Nevile Strange which we were meant to see through. But having been presented by one lot of faked evidence, it was not considered likely that we should consider a *second edition of the same thing*. And yet, if you come to look at it, all the evidence against Audrey Strange *could* be faked. The weapon taken from her fireplace, her gloves—the left hand glove dipped in blood—hidden in the ivy outside her window. The powder she uses dusted on the inside of a coat collar, and a few hairs placed there too. Her own fingerprint, occurring quite naturally on a roll of adhesive plaster taken from her room. Even the left-handed nature of the blow.

"And there was the final damning evidence of Mrs. Strange herself—I don't believe there's one of you (except the one who *knows*) who can credit her innocence after the way she behaved when we took her into custody. Practically admitted her guilt, didn't she? I mightn't have believed in her being innocent myself if it hadn't been for a private experience of my own. . . . Struck me right between the eyes it did, when I saw and heard her—because, you see, I'd known another girl who did just that very same thing, who admitted guilt when she wasn't guilty—and Audrey Strange was looking at me *with that other girl's eyes*. . . .

"I'd got to do my duty. I knew that. We police of-

ficers have to act on evidence—not on what we feel
and think. But I can tell you that at that minute I
prayed for a miracle—because I didn't see that anything but a miracle was going to help that poor lady.

"Well, I got my miracle. Got it right away!

"Mr. MacWhirter, here, turned up with his story."

He paused.

"Mr. MacWhirter, will you repeat what you told me
up at the house?"

MacWhirter turned. He spoke in short sharp sentences that carried conviction just because of their con-
ciseness.

He told of his rescue from the cliff the preceding
January and of his wish to revisit the scene. He went on.

"I went up there on Monday night. I stood there lost
in my own thoughts. It must have been, I suppose, in
the neighborhood of eleven o'clock. I looked across at
that house on the point—Gull's Point as I know it now
to be."

He paused and then went on.

"There was a rope hanging from a window of that
house into the sea. I saw a man climbing up that
rope. . . ."

Just a moment elapsed before they took it in. Mary
Aldin cried out:

"Then it *was* an outsider after all? It was nothing to
do with any of us. It was an ordinary burglar!"

"Not quite so fast," said Battle. "It was someone
who came from the other side of the river, yes, since he
swam across. But someone in the house had to have the
rope ready for him, therefore *someone inside* must have
been concerned."

He went on slowly.

"And we know of someone who was on the other
side of the river that night—someone who wasn't seen
between ten thirty and a quarter past eleven and who

might have been swimming over and back. Someone who might have a friend on this side of the water."

He added: "Eh, Mr. Latimer?"

Ted took a step backward. He cried out shrilly:

"But I can't swim! Everybody knows I can't swim. Kay, tell them I can't swim."

"Of course Ted can't swim!" Kay cried.

"Is that so?" asked Battle, pleasantly.

He moved along the boat as Ted moved in the other direction. There was some clumsy movement and a splash.

"Dear me," said Superintendent Battle in deep concern. "Mr. Latimer's gone overboard."

His hand closed like a vise on Nevile's arm as the latter was preparing to jump in after him.

"No, no, Mr. Strange. No need for you to get yourself wet. There are two of my men handy—fishing in the dinghy there." He peered over the side of the boat. "It's quite true," he said with interest. "He can't swim. It's all right. They've got him. I'll apologize presently, but really there's only one way to make quite sure that a person can't swim and that's to throw them in and watch. You see, Mr. Strange, I like to be thorough. I had to eliminate Mr. Latimer first. Mr. Royde, here, has got a groggy arm; he couldn't do any rope climbing."

Battle's voice took on a purring quality.

"So that brings us to *you*, doesn't it, Mr. Strange? A good athlete, a mountain climber, a swimmer and all that. You went over on the 10:30 ferry all right but no one can swear to seeing you at the Easterhead Hotel until a quarter past eleven in spite of your story of having been looking for Mr. Latimer then."

Nevile jerked his arm away. He threw back his head and laughed.

"You suggest that *I* swam across the river and climbed up a rope—"

"Which you had left ready hanging from your window," said Battle.

"Killed Lady Tressilian and swam back again? Why should I do such a fantastic thing? And who laid all those clues against me? I suppose *I* laid them against *myself!*"

"Exactly," said Battle. "And not half a bad idea either."

"And why should I want to kill Camilla Tressilian?"

"You didn't," said Battle. "But you did want to hang the woman who left you for another man. You're a bit unhinged mentally, you know. Have been ever since you were a child—I've looked up that old bow and arrow case by the way. Anyone who does you an injury has to be punished—and death doesn't seem to you an excessive penalty for them to pay. Death by itself wasn't enough for Audrey—*your* Audrey whom you loved—oh, yes, you loved her all right before your love turned to hate. You had to think of some special kind of death, some long-drawn-out specialized death. And when you'd thought of it, the fact that it entailed the killing of a woman who had been something like a mother to you didn't worry you in the least. . . ."

Nevile said and his voice was quite gentle:

"All lies! All lies! And I'm not mad. I'm *not* mad."

Battle said contemptuously:

"Flicked you on the raw, didn't she, when she went off and left you for another man? Hurt your vanity! To think *she* should walk out on *you*. You salved your pride by pretending to the world at large that *you'd* left *her* and you married another girl who was in love with you just to bolster up that belief. But all the time you planned what you'd do to Audrey. You couldn't think of anything worse than this—to get her hanged. A fine idea—pity you hadn't the brains to carry it out better!"

Nevile's tweed-coated shoulders moved, a queer, wriggling movement.

Battle went on:

"Childish—all that niblick stuff! Those crude trails pointing to you! Audrey must have known what you were after! She must have laughed up her sleeve! Thinking *I* didn't suspect you! You murderers are funny little fellows! So puffed up. Always thinking you've been clever and resourceful and really being quite pitifully childish. . . ."

It was a strange queer scream that came from Nevile.

"It *was* a clever idea—it *was!* You'd never have guessed. Never! Not if it hadn't been for this interfering jackanapes, this pompous Scotch fool. I'd thought out every detail—every *detail! I* can't help what went wrong. How was I to know Royde knew the truth about Audrey and Adrian? Audrey and Adrian. . . . Curse Audrey—she *shall* hang—you've *got* to hang her—I want her to die afraid—to die—to die. . . . I hate her. I tell you I want her to die. . . ."

The high whinnying voice died away. Nevile slumped down and began to cry quietly.

"Oh, God," said Mary Aldin.

She was white to the lips.

Battle said gently, in a low voice:

"I'm sorry, but I had to push him over the edge. . . . There was precious little evidence, you know."

Nevile was still whimpering. His voice was like a child's.

"*I want her to be hanged. I do want her to be hanged. . . .*"

Mary Aldin shuddered and turned to Thomas Royde. He took her hands in his.

## II

"I WAS ALWAYS frightened," said Audrey.

They were sitting on the terrace. Audrey sat close to Superintendent Battle. Battle had resumed his holiday and was at Gull's Point as a friend.

"Always frightened—all the time," said Audrey.

Battle said, nodding his head:

"I knew you were dead scared first moment I saw you. And you'd got that colorless, reserved way people have who are holding some very strong emotion in check. It might have been love or hate, but actually it was *fear*, wasn't it?"

She nodded.

"I began to be afraid of Nevile soon after we were married. But the awful thing is, you see, that I didn't know *why*. I began to think that *I* was mad."

"It wasn't you," said Battle.

"Nevile seemed to me when I married him so particularly sane and normal—always delightfully good-tempered and pleasant."

"Interesting," said Battle. "He played the part of the good sportsman, you know. That's why he could keep his temper so well at tennis. His role as a good sportsman was more important to him than winning matches. But it put a strain upon him, of course, playing a part always does. He got worse underneath."

"Underneath," whispered Audrey with a shudder. "Always *underneath*. Nothing you could get hold of. Just sometimes a word or a look and then I'd fancy I'd imagined it. . . . Something queer. And then, as I say, I thought *I* must be queer. And I went on getting more and more afraid—the kind of unreasoning fear, you know, that makes you *sick!*

"I told myself I was going mad—but I couldn't help

it. I felt I'd do anything in the world to get away! And then Adrian came and told me he loved me and I thought it would be wonderful to go away with him and be safe. . . ."

She stopped.

"You know what happened? I went off to meet Adrian —he never came . . . he was killed. . . . I felt as though Nevile had managed it somehow—"

"Perhaps he did," said Battle.

Audrey turned a startled face to him.

"Oh, do you think so?"

"We'll never know now. Motor accidents can be arranged. Don't brood on it, though, Mrs. Strange. As likely as not, it just happened naturally."

"I—I was all broken up. I went back to the Rectory— Adrian's home. We were going to have written to his mother, but as she didn't know about it, I thought I wouldn't tell her and give her pain. And Nevile came almost at once. He was very nice—and kind—and all the time I talked to him I was quite sick with fear! He said no one need know about Adrian, that I could divorce him on evidence he would send me and that he was going to remarry afterwards. I felt so thankful. I knew he had thought Kay attractive and I hoped that everything would turn out right and that I should get over this queer obsession of mine. I still thought it must be *me*.

"But I couldn't get rid of it—quite. I never felt I'd really escaped. And then I met Nevile in the Park one day and he explained that he did so want me and Kay to be friends and suggested that we should all come here in September. I couldn't refuse, how could I? After all the kind things he'd done."

" 'Will you walk into my parlor?' said the spider to the fly," remarked Superintendent Battle.

Audrey shivered.

"Yes, just that. . . ."

"Very clever he was about that," said Battle. "Protested so loudly to everyone that it was *his* idea, that everyone at once got the impression that it wasn't."

Audrey said:

"And then I got here—and it was like a kind of nightmare. I *knew* something awful was going to happen—I *knew* Nevile meant it to happen—and that it was to happen to *me. But I didn't know what it was.* I think, you know, that I nearly *did* go off my head! I was just paralyzed with fright—like you are in a dream when something's going to happen and you can't move. . . ."

"I've always thought," said Superintendent Battle, "that I'd like to have seen a snake fascinate a bird so that it can't fly away—but now I'm not so sure."

Audrey went on.

"Even when Lady Tressilian was killed, I didn't realize what it *meant.* I was puzzled. I didn't even suspect Nevile. I knew he didn't care about money—it was absurd to think he'd kill her in order to inherit fifty thousand pounds.

"I thought over and over again about Mr. Treves and the story he had told that evening. Even then I didn't connect it with Nevile. Treves had mentioned some physical peculiarity by which he could recognize the child of long ago. I've got a scar on my ear but I don't think anyone else has any sign that you'd notice."

Battle said: "Miss Aldin has a lock of white hair. Thomas Royde has a stiff right arm which might not have been only the result of an earthquake. Mr. Ted Latimer has rather an odd-shaped skull. And Nevile Strange—"

He paused.

"Surely there was no physical peculiarity about Nevile?"

"Oh, yes, there was. His left hand little finger is shorter than his right. That's very unusual, Mrs. Strange—very unusual indeed."

"So *that* was it?"

"That was it."

"And Nevile hung that sign on the lift?"

"Yes. Nipped down there and back whilst Royde and Latimer were giving the old boy drinks. Clever and simple—doubt if we could ever prove *that* was murder."

Audrey shivered again.

"Now, now," said Battle. "It's all over now, my dear. Go on talking."

"You're very clever. . . . I haven't talked so much for years!"

"No, that's what's been wrong. When did it first dawn on you what Master Nevile's game was?"

"I don't know exactly. It came to me all at once. He himself had been cleared and that left all of *us*. And then, suddenly, I saw him looking at me—a sort of gloating look. And I *knew!* That was when—"

She stopped abruptly.

"That was when what—?"

Audrey said slowly:

"When I thought a quick way out would be—best."

Superintendent Battle shook his head.

"Never give in. That's my motto."

"Oh, you're quite right. But you don't know what it does to you being afraid for so long. It paralyzes you— you can't think—you can't plan—you just wait for something awful to happen. And then, when it does happen"—she gave a sudden quick smile—"you'd be surprised at the *relief!* No more waiting and fearing— it's *come.* You'll think I'm quite demented, I suppose, if I tell you that when you came to arrest me for murder I didn't mind at all. Nevile had done his worst and it was over. I felt so safe going off with Inspector Leach."

"That's partly why we did it," said Battle. "I wanted you out of that madman's reach. And besides, if I wanted to break him down, I wanted to be able to count on the shock of the reaction. He'd seen his plan come off, as he thought—so the jolt would be all the greater."

Audrey said in a low voice:

"If he hadn't broken down, would there have been any evidence?"

"Not too much. There was MacWhirter's story of seeing a man climb up a rope in the moonlight. And there was the rope itself confirming his story, coiled up in the attic and still faintly damp. It was raining that night, you know."

He paused and stared hard at Audrey as though he were expecting her to say something.

As she merely looked interested he went on:

"And there was the pin-stripe suit. He stripped, of course, in the dark on that rocky point on the Easterhead Bay side, and thrust his suit into a niche in the rock. As it happened he put it down on a decayed bit of fish washed up by the flood tide two days ago. It made a stained patch on the shoulder—and it smelt. There was some talk, I found out, about the drains being wrong in the hotel. Nevile himself put that story about. He'd got his rain coat on over his suit, but the smell was a pervasive one. Then he got the wind up about that suit afterwards and at the first opportunity he took it off to the cleaners and, like a fool, didn't give his own name. Took a name at random, actually one he'd seen in the hotel register. That's how your friend got hold of it and, having a good head on him, he linked it up with the man climbing up the rope. You *step* on decayed fish but you don't put your *shoulder* down on it *unless you have taken your clothes off to bathe at night,* and no one would bathe for pleasure on a wet

night in September. He fitted the whole thing together.
Very ingenious man, Mr. MacWhirter."

"More than ingenious," said Audrey.

"M-m, well, perhaps. Like to know about him? I can
tell you something of his history."

Audrey listened attentively. Battle found her a good
listener.

She said:

"I owe a lot to him—and to you."

"Don't owe very much to me," said Superintendent
Battle. "If I hadn't been a fool I'd have seen the point
of that bell."

"Bell? What bell?"

"The bell in Lady Tressilian's room. Always did feel
there was something wrong about that bell. I nearly
got it, too, when I came down the stairs from the top
floor and saw one of those poles you open windows
with."

Audrey still looked bewildered.

"That was the whole point of the bell, see—to give
Nevile Strange an alibi. Lady T. didn't remember what
she had rung for—of course she didn't because *she
hadn't rung at all!* Nevile rang that bell from outside in
the passage with that long pole, the wires ran along
the ceiling. So down comes Barrett and sees Mr. Nevile
Strange go downstairs and out, and she finds Lady
Tressilian alive and well. The whole business of the
maid was fishy. What's the good of doping her for a
murder *that's going to be committed before midnight?*
Ten to one she won't have gone off properly by then.
But it fixes the murder as an inside job, and it allows
a little time for Nevile to play his role of first suspect—
then Barrett speaks and Nevile is so triumphantly cleared
that no one is going to inquire very closely as to exactly
what time he got to the hotel. We know he didn't cross
back by ferry, and no boats had been taken. There

remained the possibility of swimming. He was a powerful swimmer, but even then the time must have been
short. Up the rope he's left hanging into his bedroom
and a good deal of water on the floor, as we noticed
(but without seeing the point I'm sorry to say). Then
into his blue coat and trousers, along to Lady Tressilian's room—we won't go into that—wouldn't have
taken more than a couple of minutes, he'd fixed up that
steel ball beforehand—then back, out of his clothes,
down the rope and back to Easterhead."

"Suppose Kay had come in?"

"She'd been mildly doped, I'll bet. She was yawning
from dinner on, so they tell me. Besides he'd taken
care to have a quarrel with her so that she'd lock her
door and keep out of his way."

"I'm trying to think if I noticed the ball was gone
from the fender. I don't think I did. When did he put
it back?"

"Next morning when all the hullabaloo arose. Once
he got back in Ted Latimer's car, he had all night to
clear up his traces and fix things, mend the tennis racket,
etc. By the way, he hit the old lady *backhanded,* you
know. That's why the crime appeared to be left handed.
Strange's backhand was always his strong point, remember!"

"Don't—*don't*"—Audrey put up her hands. "I can't
bear any more."

He smiled at her.

"All the same it's done you good to talk it all out.
Mrs. Strange, may I be impertinent and give you some
advice?"

"Yes, please."

"You lived for eight years with a criminal lunatic—
that's enough to snap any woman's nerves. *But you've
got to snap out of it now, Mrs. Strange.* You don't need

to be afraid any more—and you've got to make yourself realize that."

Audrey smiled at him. The frozen look had gone from her face; it was a sweet, rather timid, but confiding face, with the wide-apart eyes full of gratitude.

"What's the best way to set about that, I wonder?"

Superintendent Battle considered.

"Think of the most difficult thing you can, and then set about doing it," he advised.


### III


ANDREW MACWHIRTER was packing.

He laid three shirts carefully in his suitcase, and then that dark blue suit which he had remembered to fetch from the cleaners. Two suits left by two different Mac-Whirters had been too much for the girl in charge.

There was a tap on the door and he called, "Come in."

Audrey Strange walked in. She said:

"I've come to thank you—are you packing?"

"Yes. I'm leaving here tonight. And sailing the day after tomorrow."

"For South America?"

"For Chile."

She said, "I'll pack for you."

He protested, but she overbore him. He watched her as she worked deftly and methodically.

"There," she said when she had finished.

"You did that well," said MacWhirter.

There was a silence. Then Audrey said:

"You saved my life. If you hadn't happened to see what you did see—"

She broke off.

Then she said:

"Did you realize at once, that night on the cliff when you—you stopped me going over—when you said, 'Go home, I'll see that you're not hanged'—did you realize *then* that you'd got some important evidence?"

"Not precisely," said MacWhirter. "I had to think it out."

"Then how could you say—what you did say?"

MacWhirter always felt annoyed when he had to explain the intense simplicity of his thought processes.

"I meant just precisely that—that I intended to prevent you from being hanged."

The color came up in Audrey's cheeks.

"Supposing I had done it."

"That would have made no difference."

"Did you think I *had* done it, then?"

"I did not speculate upon the matter overmuch. I was inclined to believe you were innocent, but it would have made no difference to my course of action."

"And then you remembered the man on the rope?"

MacWhirter was silent for a few minutes. Then he cleared his throat.

"You may as well know, I suppose. I did not actually see a man climbing up a rope—indeed I could not have done so, for I was up on Stark Head on Sunday night, not on Monday. I deduced what must have happened from the evidence of the suit and my suppositions were confirmed by the finding of a wet rope in the attic."

From red Audrey had gone white. She said incredulously:

"Your story was all a lie?"

"Deductions would not have carried weight with the police. I had to say I *saw* what happened."

"But—you might have had to swear to it at my trial."

"Yes."

"You would have done that?"

"I would."

Audrey cried:

"And you—you are the man who lost his job and came down to throwing himself off a cliff because he wouldn't tamper with the truth!"

"I have a great regard for the truth. But I've discovered there are things that matter more."

"Such as?"

"You," said MacWhirter.

Audrey's eyes dropped. He cleared his throat in an embarrassed manner.

"There's no need for you to feel under a great obligation or anything of that kind. You'll never hear of me again after today. The police have got Strange's confession and they'll not need my evidence. In any case I hear he's so bad he'll maybe not live to come to trial."

"I'm glad of that," said Audrey.

"You were fond of him once?"

"Of the man I thought he was."

MacWhirter nodded.

"We've all felt that way, maybe."

He went on.

"Everything's turned out well. Superintendent Battle was able to act upon my story and break down the man—"

Audrey interrupted. She said:

"He worked upon your story, yes. But I don't believe you fooled him. He deliberately shut his eyes."

"Why do you say that?"

"When he was talking to me he mentioned it was lucky you saw what you did in the moonlight, and then added something—a sentence or two later—about it being *a rainy night*."

MacWhirter was taken aback.

"That's true. On Monday night I doubt if I'd have seen anything at all."

"It doesn't matter," said Audrey.

"He knew that what you pretended to have seen was what had really happened. But it explains why he worked on Nevile to break him down. He suspected Nevile as soon as Thomas told him about me and Adrian. He knew then that if he was right about the kind of crime—he had fixed on the wrong person—what he wanted was some kind of evidence to use on Nevile. He wanted, as he said, a miracle—you were Superintendent Battle's answer to prayer."

"That's a curious thing for him to say," said MacWhirter dryly.

"So you see," said Audrey, "you are a miracle. My special miracle."

MacWhirter said earnestly:

"I'd not like you to feel you're under an obligation to me. I'm going right out of your life—"

"Must you?" said Audrey.

He stared at her. The color came up, flooding her ears and temples.

She said:

"Won't you take me with you?"

"You don't know what you're saying!"

"Yes, I do. I'm doing something very difficult—but something that matters to me more than life or death. I know the time is very short. By the way, I'm conventional, I should like to be married before we go!"

"Naturally," said MacWhirter, deeply shocked. "You don't imagine I'd suggest anything else."

"I'm sure you wouldn't," said Audrey.

MacWhirter said:

"I'm not your kind. I thought you'd marry that quiet fellow who's cared for you so long."

"Thomas? Dear true Thomas. He's too true. He's

faithful to the image of a girl he loved years ago. But the person he really cares for is Mary Aldin, though he doesn't know it yet himself."

MacWhirter took a step towards her. He spoke sternly.

"Do you mean what you're saying?"

"Yes . . . I want to be with you always, never to leave you. If you go, I shall never find anybody like you, and I shall go sadly all my days."

MacWhirter sighed. He took out his wallet and carefully examined its contents.

He murmured:

"A special license comes expensive. I'll need to go to the bank first thing tomorrow."

"I could lend you some money," murmured Audrey.

"You'll do nothing of the kind. If I marry a woman, I pay for the license. You understand?"

"You needn't," said Audrey softly, "look so stern."

He said gently as he came towards her,

"Last time I had my hands on you, you felt like a bird—struggling to escape. You'll never escape now. . . ."